AMBITION

AMBITION

A NOVEL BY
KATE BRIAN

SIMON PULSE
New York   London   Toronto   Sydney

SIMON PULSE

An imprint of Simon & Schuster Children's Publishing Division
1230 Avenue of the Americas, New York, NY 10020

alloy**entertainment**

Produced by Alloy Entertainment
151 West 26th Street, New York, NY 10001

Typography by Andrea C. Uva
The text of this book was set in Filosofia.

Manufactured in the United States of America
First Simon Pulse edition May 2008

2 4 6 8 10 9 7 5 3

Library of Congress Control Number 2008921695

ISBN-13: 978-1-4169-5882-6
ISBN-10: 1-4169-5882-7

This one's for all the readers who have e-mailed me with their encouraging words, keen questions, and even keener insight. It's incredible to know that this series has such dedicated and intelligent fans. Keep it coming!

A DEAL

I sat in the front row of folding chairs in the Great Room of Mitchell Hall and stared at the gray, unfeeling faces that hovered over the long table before me. The gray faces that would decide my fate. Our fate.

The fate of Billings House.

They were all against us. I could feel it, right in the pit of my gut—this torturous sensation like some large rodent was kicking in my stomach, gnawing greedily at my heart and lungs. And as if the vociferous organ-muncher wasn't enough, I was also in pain. Real pain. My lungs were raw from inhaling tons of smoke in the underground tunnel outside Gwendolyn Hall, the remnants of the charred building still billowing plumes into the air at the edge of Easton Academy's campus. My face hurt as if it had been repeatedly and mercilessly slapped. My head was being intermittently pierced by an invisible ice pick. My eyes were so dry that every time I blinked, my lids stuck to them for one brief, excruciating moment before popping wide open again. I tried not to close them, but that just made them drier.

This was my punishment, my penance for last night. For sneaking out and going to the Legacy instead of staying home with Josh. For downing all those frothy pink drinks. For hooking up with my best friend's boyfriend. For breaking the heart of the guy I loved. The only guy I had ever truly loved.

Josh was behind me somewhere in the expectant crowd. The whole school had gathered to hear what would become of Billings. The anticipation in the air was so thick I could feel its warmth on my neck.

Or maybe that was just Constance Talbot's panicked breathing. Either way, my heart started to pound as Headmaster Cromwell finished listing the grievances against Billings. I had already lost Josh. I couldn't lose Billings. Not now. Billings House was my home. I needed my home.

"These infractions are grievous," Headmaster Cromwell said. His white hair was perfectly coiffed, his square jaw as imperious as ever, but under the harsh fluorescents I could see every crag in his face, every wrinkle. He lifted a page of stark white paper and read from it. "Hazing, initiation ceremonies, fighting, ignoring curfew on several occasions—"

"But that wasn't us. That was all Cheyenne," London Simmons complained under her breath, as if she and most of the rest of my friends hadn't gone right along with all of it. London sat a few seats to my left, next to Vienna Clark, to whom she was always attached at the hip. They wore matching black suits as if they were attending a funeral. Although no decent person would ever show that much cleavage at a funeral.

"Ignoring my strict mandate to remain on campus the night of Sunday, October thirty-first," Cromwell continued. "And, most egregious, destruction of school property." He laid the paper down and laced his fingers together on top of it. "Destruction of one of the oldest buildings on this campus," he reiterated, looking me dead in the eye.

Me. Of course me. President of Billings. Two days ago, most people in this room would have said that as president of the most sought-after dorm on campus, I was the most blessed of the blessed. Today I was the most loathed of the loathed. It wasn't like I'd pulled a crazy Mrs. Rochester and run through Gwendolyn with a lit torch, cackling as I burned the place to the ground. The fire had been a result of London and Vienna's toking tour of Easton. Someone had left a burning joint behind, and it hadn't been me. But even as my cheeks stung at the unfairness of being singled out, I realized the situation was dire. When our crimes were compiled that way, they sounded really, really awful.

"Like we were the only ones at Gwendolyn," Noelle Lange said under her breath. For all her partying the night before, Noelle looked as perfect as ever in a crisp white shirt and gray wide-leg pants, her long brown hair pulled back in a tortoiseshell headband. In jeans and a black cashmere sweater she had given me a few weeks back, I felt troll-like in her presence. I wriggled back in my seat and endeavored to sit up straight. Endeavored to meet Cromwell's cool stare with my own.

"Headmaster Cromwell?" London blurted, standing up in her four-inch heels. "I just want to point out that we weren't the only ones there last night," she said, glancing at Noelle for backup. "I mean, the guys were there too, and—"

"I don't believe I opened the floor to comments, Miss Simmons," Headmaster Cromwell said, leaning so close to his microphone that his voice blasted through the suspended corner speakers like the voice of God. London let out a yip of surprise and sat right back down.

"Now, where was I?"

As Cromwell sifted through his papers, Constance leaned in close to my ear from behind. "Whit talked to his grandmother, and she said they're going to deal with the other students individually, but since our whole dorm was there, they're viewing it as an overarching house problem and they're going to, quote, 'deal with Billings accordingly.'"

Whit was Walt Whittaker, Constance's older boyfriend, whose grandmother sat on the Easton board, which meant she was one of the gray faces judging us. But right then the diminutive old woman looked like she was starting to doze off at the far end of the table. My life was on the line and she was catnapping. Real nice. Meanwhile, Susan Llewelyn, the Billings alumna who sat on the board—the woman who had sent us to the secret passage in Gwendolyn Hall—was nowhere to be found. Her seat at the table was empty.

"I am S.N.S.," Portia Ahronian said, rolling her big green eyes. "So not surprised," she clarified. "The Crom has been trying to find a way to get rid of us from D-one. He may be acting all stern and appalled, but you know he's L.O.T.I."

Headmaster Cromwell cleared his throat loudly.

"Well, with a list of infractions this long, a vote seems superfluous," Cromwell said. "But the school bylaws dictate that we must vote. So, the directive on the table is this: Shall the board of directors hereby dissolve Billings House and redistribute its members throughout the remaining girls' dormitories? Yay or nay? All those in favor—"

My pulse pounded in my temples, my eyes, my throat. They were going to do it. They were going to take our home away.

"This isn't happening," Rose Sakowitz mumbled.

"They can't close Billings. I just got in," Lorna Gross whined.

Sabine DuLac leaned forward, grasping the back of my chair. "Do something," she whispered urgently. "Reed, you have to do something."

"Wait!" I was on my feet. My voice reverberated off the high ceiling of the Great Room, the largest gathering space on campus aside from the cafeteria and the chapel. Dead silence enveloped the room as everyone gaped at me. Dead silence as hundreds of faces blurred before my heavy, hungover eyes.

"Yes, Miss Brennan?" Headmaster Cromwell said, his upper lip curled in distaste.

At least he hadn't used his godlike voice to cut me down too. That was something. Unfortunately, I had no idea what I was going to say next.

"This . . . this isn't fair," I stated, sounding unresolved, even to myself. My querulous words were met with snickers around the room. I hadn't meant to whine, but whine I had. I took a deep breath and tried again. "With all due respect, Headmaster Cromwell, you haven't given us a chance," I said, trying for a more authoritative tone.

I saw a few people sit forward in their seats, intrigued, including towheaded freshman Amberly Carmichael and her friends, who had a vested interest in keeping Billings open. Noelle and I had, after all, promised that they would get in to the house their junior year if they caused a diversion so we could sneak off campus the night before, and they had come through. From what I'd heard, they had staged the most convincing and violent catfight in the history of Easton, drawing security personnel and Headmaster Cromwell to their dorm, right when we needed them to.

"Haven't I?" Cromwell sniffed and looked down at his all-important papers. "I believe you and your housemates have had plenty of chances."

His dismissive attitude shot right under my skin, and I felt a surge of adrenaline take over.

"No, sir, we have not," I replied firmly, earning a few surprised murmurs from my peers. They couldn't believe I was standing up to Cromwell like this. Honestly, neither could I, but I kept going. "I'm the first to admit that things at Billings have been pretty terrible this year. But in case you've forgotten, one of our best friends just died. And yeah, okay, maybe we're having a hard time dealing with that right now, but Billings has been an asset to this school in the past and it will be again. You just have to give us a chance to prove it."

My friends in the front two rows all sat up a bit straighter, held their heads a bit higher. A flutter of pride tickled my chest. My speech was working. On them, at least.

"And how, exactly, are you going to do that?" Headmaster Cromwell asked, leaning his weight on his forearms as he eyed me expectantly.

Oh. Right. I should have had a "how" ready here. I turned to look at the Billings Girls, widening my eyes in desperation and praying one of them had an answer. Noelle cleared her throat and brought her hand down to her side where she surreptitiously rubbed her fingers together.

Money. Of course. Money talked around here. Louder than just about anything else. But how much money? I knew what a lot of cash was to me—a scholarship student from a lower-middle-class family with one car and two mortgages—but how many zeros did I need to add to impress people who paid for plastic surgery for their dogs and had personal chefs to toast their French bread?

"We'll hold a fund-raiser," I announced. "Billings will pledge to raise . . . one million dollars for Easton."

Gasps and whispered filled the room.

"If we succeed, Billings stays as is," I continued, on firmer footing now. "If we fail, you can do what you want with us."

Cromwell's sharp blue eyes narrowed. He covered his microphone with one hand and turned to whisper to the gentleman next to him. Soon the whole board was playing a game of telephone, each whispering to the next and on down the line. Finally, their comments made it back to Cromwell and he cleared his throat. I held my breath. Everyone in the room held their breath.

Slowly, Cromwell leaned toward the microphone. It was impossible to read his expression. Possibly because he had only one—annoyed.

Please. Please don't take this away from me. Not now.

"Make it five million, Miss Brennan," he said with a small but devilish smile, "and you have a deal."

"Yes!" someone behind me cheered. The room erupted in conversation and squeaking chairs, but all I could see was that number. Five million. A huge number. An impossible number.

"We can do that, no problem," Vienna said, clapping her hands happily.

"Silence!" Headmaster Cromwell's voice boomed through the speakers once more.

He got his silence.

"There is one stipulation," he said, looking at the Billings section. "This five million dollars must be *raised,* not gleaned from your trust funds or borrowed from your parents. You must actually raise it, and you must raise it in one month's time. I will also be contacting the Billings alumni and making it clear to them that they are not to help you with the preparations for whatever you conjure up. This fundraiser will be planned by you and paid for by you, and any profit will be fairly earned. Is that understood?"

Suddenly, my friends were no longer cheering. I turned to look at them. They couldn't back out on me now. I'd gotten us a reprieve. I'd taken a stand. *Please don't make me look like an idiot now.*

Portia glanced at the Twin Cities. Vienna whispered something over her shoulder to Shelby Wordsworth. Rose bent in conversation with Tiffany Goulbourne and Astrid Chou. Everyone conferred while I stood there and waited. Finally, they all faced forward and Portia nodded confidently. I faced the board, looked Cromwell in the eye, and smiled.

"Done."

NEW FOCUS

"Reed, seriously, have you ever considered a career as a politician?" Tiffany asked as we emerged from Mitchell Hall into the crisp, cold New England air. The sky over Easton Academy was a shade of blue so bright it looked almost fake, and orange and yellow leaves chased one another across the cobblestone path in front of us. Tiffany wrapped her white coat closer to her tall body and flipped up the collar so that it grazed the smooth ebony skin of her cheeks. How could she look so perfect today, when I felt as if I had been run over repeatedly by a monster truck?

"Um, no," I replied.

"Well, maybe you should." Astrid nudged me with her elbow as the wind tossed her short dark hair. She wore a colorful plaid skirt over hot pink tights and purple shoes, her eye makeup colors chosen to match her lower half. "That was bloody brilliant."

"Amazing," Sabine agreed with sheer admiration in her eyes. "Headmaster Cromwell didn't see that coming at all."

"Agreed. If you pull this off, you will go down in history as the president who saved Billings," Shelby said. Her leather-gloved fingers moved swiftly over her iPhone's touch pad as she checked for texts. Shelby had a sophisticated air that made her seem like she was in her mid-twenties instead of her late teens. She wore a double-breasted brown tweed coat; her blond hair hung in loose waves around her face; and she held her chin slightly up, as if her photo might be snapped at any moment.

"Yeah, or the last," Missy Thurber put in with a sniff of her wide nostrils. Her comment earned her a whack on the back of her blond head from Portia. "Ow! Was that necessary?"

"Neg the neg," Portia ordered, shoving her hands into the pockets of her cropped fur jacket. "We need positive thinking from here on out, right, Reed?"

"Exactly," I said with a nod. I decided right then and there that I was going to be Shelby's version of a Billings president rather than Missy's. From now on, I would focus all my energy on this fund-raiser and on saving Billings.

Besides, it wasn't like I would have much else to do now that Josh had made it clear that we were over.

My heart constricted as fuzzy flashes of last night suddenly assaulted my brain. Dash McCafferty's lips on mine. Josh's face when he found us in that private tent. The way he'd practically spat in my face as he told me it was over. How could someone who supposedly loved me so much look at me that way? And how was my heart ever going to heal when every time I thought about Josh, it broke a little more?

"Are you all right?" Noelle asked me. "You just went all *visage blanc*."

I blinked and tried to look normal. It wasn't like I could confide in Noelle about what had happened. After all, she and Dash had gotten back together last night, and she had no clue that I'd gotten horizontal with him. Had no idea that this indiscretion was the cause of my breakup with Josh. All I had told her was that Josh had ended it out of nowhere. Big, big lie.

"I'm fine. Just an adrenaline crash," I told her.

"Reed!" Amberly shouted, hustling over to me with her two ever-present lackeys at her sides. Her loose blond curls bounced around her angelic face and she wore a light pink coat with a white-and-pink plaid scarf over white thin-wale cords. As matchy-matchy as ever. "We just wanted to let you know that if you need any help with the fund-raiser—anything whatsoever—we're here for you," she said, clasping my arm.

"Thanks," I said vaguely. "I'll keep that in mind."

I turned around to search the crowd for Josh. Maybe I'd focus on saving Billings after I talked to him. I had to talk to him. Had to try to explain. Try to make things right. Try . . . something.

Most of the student body had divided into klatches that now dotted the lawn around Mitchell Hall. Gage Coolidge, Trey Prescott, and some other guys from Ketlar Hall stood about ten feet away, huddled together against the cold, since guys were too cool for outerwear, but Josh wasn't with them. Then, from the corner of my eye, I spotted him. Alone. Head down. Skulking toward the edge of campus. Toward the Jonathan Arthur Montgomery Building, which housed the art studios, the *Chronicle* newspaper office, the literary magazine office, practice rooms for the choir and orchestra, and several other venues for artistic pursuits. The J.A.M. Building was one of Josh's two favorite spots on campus, the other being the art cemetery, where we used to rendezvous before he rendezvoused there with Cheyenne.

God, that seemed like ages ago. When Cheyenne was alive, when I had caught her trysting with my boyfriend, when I had almost lost him over her. A lot had happened this year. So much had changed. And it was only the first of November.

"Reed? Where are you going?" Noelle asked me as I turned away from my friends. "We have a lot to do if we're going to make this fundraiser happen."

I paused. "I know. I just have something I have to take care of."

One step away and a dark blue sweater blocked my path. I looked up. Hovering over me was an unreasonably tall guy with brown eyes and a preppy haircut that screamed Young Wall Street.

Weston Bright. West for short. Ketlar Hall. Senior. Lacrosse captain.

My brain recited these things, though why it knew them or cared, I had no idea.

"Reed, what you did in there . . . that was amazing," West said, speaking the first words he'd ever spoken to me. He pushed his hand into the pocket of his gray slacks. His smile was genuine, affable. "How'd you do that? I think if I tried to stand up to Cromwell, I'd keel over drooling."

"I don't know," I replied, glancing at Josh's disappearing form.
I really didn't know. Considering everything I'd been through in the
past twenty-four hours, I should have been curled up in a ball somewhere, babbling incoherently.

"Maybe we can get together sometime and you can float some
theories," West suggested. "I wouldn't mind a few tips before my
college interviews."

I blinked at him. He was asking me out. This unusually tall person and his preppy hair were asking me out. The near corpse of my
relationship with Josh was, I hoped, still revivable, and this guy was
asking me out. How did he even know Josh and I had broken up? I
had only told the Billings Girls. Was Josh spreading the word? Was he
so psyched about his newfound freedom that he was shouting it from
rooftops everywhere?

"Um, maybe. Can we talk about this later?"

"Sure. What's your number? I'll text you," West said. He typed in
my phone number and gave me a smile before sauntering off.

"Wow, Reed," London said, sidling over to give me a hip-nudge. She
looked West's departing form up and down like he was a piece of meat
and tossed her thick, artificially streaked hair over her shoulder. "Way
to bounce back."

"Are you kidding me?" I hissed at her. "I just broke up with Josh.
I'm not just going to start dating."

"Who said anything about dating?" London replied. "Just hook
up with the guy. West is an excellent kisser," she said, smiling at him
over my shoulder.

I glanced back there as well.

"Ew," I said, realizing that London knew from experience. "I have to go."

There was only one guy I was interested in right now. The one fleeing the scene—my scene—as fast as his Dsquared sneakers would carry him.

TELL ME HOW YOU REALLY FEEL

As I approached the art studio, I couldn't ever remember feeling so nervous in my life. Not when I'd first arrived at Easton. Not when I had been questioned by the police about Thomas Pearson's murder last year. Not when I thought I was about to be expelled. Maybe on the Billings rooftop last winter when Ariana had been hell-bent on throwing me over the side. But that had been more terror than nervousness. A trembling, knee-weakening, life-flashing-before-my-eyes kind of terror.

This was almost worse. Because there was hope behind these nerves. Hope even though I knew I was about to get crushed. But I couldn't seem to squelch it, even to protect myself.

I pressed my damp palms into my jeans, then grasped the cold door handle and pulled. Perched on a wooden stool, Josh sat with his back curled like a *C*. So lonely and sad. He didn't look up from his easel. On the canvas was a charcoal profile that looked a lot like mine.

He hadn't opened any paints yet. The brushes sat dry and untouched. When he finally turned and saw me there, anger flashed through his blue eyes.

"You can't be here," he said.

"Why not? Maybe I've developed an interest in painting." I tried for levity. Bad idea.

Josh stood up, nearly knocking his seat over. "No. I mean, you can't *really* be here. You can't actually think we're going to talk about this. That you're going to find some way to explain it that will make me forgive you."

All the oxygen left the room. *Tell me how you really feel.*

"Josh, please—"

"No! Reed, no. God!" He brought his hand to his head and winced. "I can't get the picture of you and Dash out of my mind. Do you have any idea what this is like for me?"

"Actually, yeah. I do," I snapped without thinking. The picture of Cheyenne straddling him on the love seat in the Art Cemetery came screeching back in full Technicolor, as did the gut-wrenching horror of how it had felt to watch it all unfold. "But I took you back, remember?"

Josh's face screwed up in disgust. "You took me back because it wasn't me there with her. Because she drugged me. Because I didn't know what I was doing."

He had me there. I was drunk last night, but I had known what I was doing. Had flirted with the idea of doing it for months. How could something that had seemed so right and harmless less than eighteen hours ago now be such an obvious mistake? Why hadn't I realized that if I let Dash pull me onto that mattress, if I let him touch me the way he had, that I would be here now—my heart in pieces, Josh's heart in pieces, wishing there was any way in hell I could take it all back?

What could I say?

"Josh, I love you," I attempted. "I—"

"Don't," he spat. "Of all things, do not say that."

The venom in his voice stopped me cold. That was all it took. All it took for me to realize that this was a lost cause. That Josh was lost to me. Forever.

All I wanted was for him to hug me. To tell me that everything was going to be okay. To be my rock. He had always been that for me. Whenever I screwed up or everything around me seemed to be falling apart, Josh had made it better. But he couldn't make this better, because this time my screwup had hurt *him*. I had deprived myself of my one true comfort in life, and the realization gouged my heart out.

"Please, just go," he said, his shoulders slumping. "Just leave me alone."

"Fine." My voice, my eyes, my throat, were filled with tears as I took a step back. Away from him. "Fine, I'll go."

And I started to. I did. But then, out of nowhere, a terrifying thought occurred to me. A thought that somehow, in all the emotional wreckage, had never even been a glimmer until now. And it stopped me in my tracks. Cold dread overcame me.

Josh was so angry. So hurt. What if he . . .

I couldn't say it. But I had to. I had to beg for mercy. One last favor. For old time's sake?

A lump the size of an orange blocked my windpipe, trying to tell me this was a bad idea. But my fear of what might happen if I didn't speak overcame my conscience. "Josh, I have to ask you one thing," I said, my voice thick.

"What?" He glanced at me.

"You're not . . . I mean . . . you're not going to tell Noelle, are you? About me and Dash?" I asked.

Josh looked at me for a moment, then shook his head and laughed. He laughed so bitterly, I'm not even sure the noise he made could be categorized as a laugh. My heart felt sick. I knew what he thought of me right then and I hated myself. But now that he'd left me, I needed Noelle more than ever.

"No," he said finally, looking at me like I was the crusty scum that formed on the outer rims of his paint jars. "No, I won't tell your precious Noelle. If that's what you really care about here, then don't worry. Your slutty little secret is safe with me."

Tears spilled down my face. Coming from Josh—from someone who was normally so kind and levelheaded and understanding—the words couldn't have stung more. But at least I knew he would keep my secret. He was the most decent, honest guy I knew. However awful his wording was, the promise was just as strong.

"Josh—"

"Good luck saving Billings," he said with a sneer.

His silent message? *I hope you fail.*

Then he turned his back on me, and I knew it was for good this time.

I had to get out of there. Now. I turned and ran for the door, holding one hand over my mouth to keep the sobs in check. As I stumbled into the hallway, I nearly took out Ivy Slade in her white-and-black plaid cape. Perfect. She was so the person I wanted to see right now.

Her blue eyes like ice, Ivy shot me a derisive look, then peered past me through the glass pane in the classroom door. Her thin, dark eyebrows arched and she crossed her slim arms over her chest. Her dangling silver earrings swung, catching on strands of her sleek, black hair.

"Trouble in paradise?" she asked. "Just think, if you hadn't crashed my party last night, none of this would have happened."

Her party. As if the Legacy belonged to her. It was an ages-old tradition, and she had tried to claim it as her own, changing the rules and ostracizing all the Easton Academy legacies. Maybe I had crashed it, but I'd only done it because I was trying to help my fellow Easton students get what was rightfully theirs. And, okay, I was also trying to have a little fun. That, of course, had not happened. At least not after the first couple hours of drinking and dancing. After that, it had all gone to hell.

"Haven't you ever heard that it's inadvisable to have major relationship status conversations after chugging several fuzzy navels?" she asked slyly.

She was taking pleasure in this, and she wasn't even trying to hide it.

"How do you know what I was drinking?" I demanded.

"Oh, I make a habit of keeping an eye on party crashers, just in case they decide to cause trouble," Ivy said, tilting her head. "Luckily, you only caused trouble for yourself."

She placed a hand on the doorknob behind her. Josh was in there. She was about to join Josh. My heart skipped a nervous, covetous beat.

"What the hell are you doing here?" I demanded.

"Working on my senior project." She glanced over her shoulder again, smoothing her shiny hair with her long, pale fingers. "I'll be spending a lot of time in the studio this year," she added pointedly.

Implication? *With Josh. I'll be spending a lot of time in the studio this year with Josh.*

She was just like Cheyenne with her "seniors stick together" routine. All to spend time with Josh. And just like that, I remembered. Ivy's room last night. That bizarre collage. The pictures of her and Cheyenne being BFFs on beaches and boats and tennis courts. Ivy and Cheyenne, who were supposed to hate each other. Why had they hidden their friendship from the world? And what else was Ivy hiding?

"Well, I should go. Let you get back to your little fund-raising project," Ivy said. "It's good to have a distraction at a trying time like this, Reed. Doctor Phil would be proud."

She gave my shoulder a quick squeeze with faux sympathy, then turned and walked into the room where Josh sat. Her red lips stretched into a mocking grin right before she slammed the heavy door in my face.

The tears burst forth all over again. I ran down the hall toward the exit, but before I could get through the door, it was opening. I slammed into someone so hard he was knocked off his feet and his stuff scattered everywhere. Who knew the J.A.M. Building was so heavily trafficked on Monday evenings?

"Dammit," I said, automatically crouching to the ground. Tears streaked down my nose, mingling with snot. I wiped my hand across my face, not even sure whether it made a difference. "I'm so sorry."

"No. It's my fault," my victim replied, gathering his bag and notebook. "I never look where I'm going. Hey, are you okay?" I looked in his face for the first time. Light brown skin, dark, floppy hair, concerned brown eyes. Light brown eyes. Odd. Nice.

"M'fine," I mumbled. "Just have to get out of here."

"Okay." He stood up, repositioning his stuff as it slid in his hands "I'm Marcellus Alberro. Marc for short. And you're Reed Brennan."

I looked at him quizzically. Why he felt the need to tell me my name was beyond me.

"Yeah."

"I thought it was so cool how you didn't back down from Cromwell," Marc said with a smile.

I immediately thought of my encounter with West. Damn. Was this guy going to use my so-called bravery as a segue to ask me out too?

"I'm gonna do a story about it for the *Chronicle*," he told me. "I was actually just on my way up to the offices to do some research and see if they've ever tried to shut down a whole dorm like this before. I'm on the paper," he added needlessly. "In case that wasn't clear."

I heard myself laugh, which was a surprise.

"Well, good luck with your story, Marc-For-Short," I said, shoving the door open and letting the cold air pour in. All I wanted to do was go back to my dorm and do that curling-up-in-a-ball thing.

"Thanks. I'd like to interview you for it, if I could," he blurted.

"Now?" I asked.

"Now's good. If you can."

Couldn't he see what a mess I was? I was in no shape to be interviewed. But still, maybe it was a good idea. Get the press behind us. Some free publicity. Another distraction.

"Actually, I—"

But Ivy's laughter cut me short. It wafted down the hallway from the studio, through the air vents, along the walls. It was everywhere. And it made the hair on my arms stand on end. Josh had made her laugh. Angry, bitter, brokenhearted Josh was down there right now, making Ivy Slade laugh.

"I'm sorry. I have to go," I said.

Letting the door bang behind me, I tore across the rapidly darkening campus, leaving an understandably confused Marc-For-Short Alberro behind.

BLACKBALLED

I had to call Dash. He was, after all, the reason I was such a total mess. I had risked everything for him, and now that I knew that I had risked and lost, I had to know why. Why had he lured me up to the roof at the Legacy? Why had he begged me to be with him? Why, when he was still in love with Noelle? Why, when all along he was planning on getting back together with her?

Or had he already? Had he gotten back together with her before we had hooked up? The idea sent my pulse into panic-attack mode as I rushed through the dark to Billings. I had to know. After everything that had happened, I deserved some kind of explanation. I knew now that I'd been used, but I was not at all blameless. I needed to know how awful my infraction was when it came to Noelle. Had I simply hooked up with a friend's ex right before they had gotten back together, or had I helped the guy cheat on said friend?

There was a big difference.

"Reed! Wait up! Hold the door!" someone shouted as I slid my electronic key through the slot next to the inner door to Billings. The outer door was slowly closing as Kiki Rosen managed to slip through.

"Hey. Thanks," she said, breathless. "I lost my key."

"You did?" I asked.

"Yeah, over the weekend. Probably somewhere between here and Boston. I gotta go to Hell Hall tomorrow and get a new one. Such a pain in the ass," she said, tugging the earbuds from her ears. I could hear tinny guitar music and drums blaring through them. She hustled inside and headed straight for the parlor off the Billings lobby, where a few people were hanging out.

"You coming?" she asked over her shoulder as she struggled out of her puffer coat. "Astrid said we were going to talk fund-raiser."

"In a minute. I have to do something first," I replied.

I sprinted up the stairs before anyone could protest, taking the steps two at a time. My room on the top floor was, mercifully, empty. Sitting on the edge of my bed, I struggled to get my breathing under control as I speed-dialed Dash on my iPhone. I held my breath, unsure of what I was going to say, but certain it was going to be shouted. I had a lot of angry, confused adrenaline to spew. Why not spew it at Dash "You're All I Think About, Reed" McCafferty?

The phone rang once, then clicked over to voice mail.

"This is Dash McCafferty. Please leave a message and I'll get back to you as soon as I can."

So formal, that Dash. I hung up before the beep. I was not in the frame of mind to leave a coherent message. I yanked my laptop off my desk and hit a few keys to bring it to life. My fingers trembled as they hovered over the keyboard, waiting for my e-mail to boot up. When it did, I typed a simple message.

Dash,
We need to talk. Call me.
—Reed

Message sent, I tossed the computer on the foot of my bed and collapsed backward, my legs hooked over the side of my mattress, feet on the floor. Dried tears tightened my cheeks. Josh hated me. Hated me. And Dash had abandoned me. And Noelle was going to kill me when she found out. How had I gotten here? How had everything gotten so screwed up? My head pounded as if my brain were pulsating against my skull and my skull against my skin. I took a deep breath, closed my eyes, and brought my fingers to my temples.

Breathe, Reed. Just breathe.

But Josh's disgusted expression kept flitting through my brain and my head pounded harder. My throat was desiccated, and the muscles in my back and neck coiled painfully. I couldn't take it anymore. This wasn't just the drama talking. This was the hangover. The lack of sleep. I had been awake since yesterday morning. Awake and partying and drinking and puking and barely eating a thing.

God, I loathed myself.

It was still early. Not even six o'clock. Dinner had yet to be served at the dining hall, but I didn't care. This day had to end. Now. I would take something for the headache and go to bed, and tomorrow I would start fresh. Start my life without Josh. Somehow, I would start over.

I forced myself up to a seated position, my eye sockets exploding with pain, and reached for my top desk drawer, where I kept a small bottle of Tylenol. As I yanked the drawer open there was a racket not unlike the sound of a dozen bowling balls racing down their lanes. Then a slam.

The unexpected noise scared me half to death, but when I peered into the drawer, my heart all but stopped.

Black marbles, dozens of them, had rolled forward from the back of the drawer and slammed into the front. A few latecomers still trickled forth, bouncing around my pens and pencils to join their friends.

Black marbles. Used in the inner circle for voting people out. For expelling people from Billings.

Who had put these in my drawer? Why? Was it just some kind of stupid prank, or was someone sending a message? That they wanted me out? Wanted me gone?

I was just starting to hyperventilate when the door to my room opened. I grabbed the Tylenol bottle, then slammed the drawer so hard the framed picture of me and my brother, Scott, fell over on my desktop. Sabine came traipsing in, all excitement, too hyper to realize anything was wrong.

"Omigosh! Everyone on campus is talking about how incredible you were," she trilled, dropping her backpack on her bed. She turned to me, her green eyes glowing. Lately Sabine had updated her Caribbean wardrobe to better suit the New England autumn weather, and today she was wearing a kelly green turtleneck, tartan skirt, and tall brown boots. The preppy look suited her, but she still wore her shell earrings, which dangled almost to her shoulders. "Your fund-raiser is *the* hot topic of the day. Do you have any ideas yet?"

"No. Not yet," I said shakily.

I popped the top off the Tylenol bottle with my thumb and let it fall to the floor. The two white pills lodged for a second in my dry throat, but I managed to choke them down.

"Do you want some water or something?" Sabine asked.

"M'fine," I mumbled. I kicked off my sneakers and tipped to the side so I could free my covers from under my butt without actually standing up.

"You're going to bed?" Sabine asked, her face falling. "But everyone's waiting for you downstairs to talk about the fund-raiser."

"Tomorrow," I told her, clicking off my desk light.

I lay down fully clothed and pulled the covers up over my head, turning my back on her crestfallen face—on my desk and everything it contained. All I wanted was to go to sleep and put the past two days behind me.

Suddenly, I felt her weight at the foot of my bed. I looked up to find Sabine sitting near my feet, looking at me with concern in the dim light coming through the window.

"Is it Josh? Do you want to talk about it?" she asked.

"Not now," I replied.

"Because I know it's hard, having your heart broken," she said sympathetically.

"Who broke your heart?" I muttered. There was the tiniest light of curiosity deep inside of me. Sabine had never mentioned any exes before.

"Me? Oh, no one. I've never had a real boyfriend," she told me, looking down at her hands. "But I helped my sister through a horrible breakup. She said she would never have survived it if it wasn't for me. So maybe I can help you, too."

I managed a tight smile for her benefit. "Maybe. Just not tonight, okay? Right now all I want to do is sleep."

"Okay," Sabine said finally. "I'll go tell them."

"Thanks."

Sabine slipped out and closed the door with a quiet click. Part of me felt guilty for bailing on my friends, but it was just one night. I could think about all of this tomorrow—about the fund-raiser and the black marbles and Dash and Noelle and Josh and Ivy and everything else. Right now, I craved only the sweet release of sleep.

HUNTER BRADEN

The black marbles were still there in the morning. I had hoped to find when I woke up that they were just one of the many sick, swirling dreams I had all night long, but when I opened the drawer, there they were. Not a figment of my subconscious, but real. Unwilling to dwell on the circumstances of how they had gotten there, I gathered them all up, shoved them into a lone sock that had lost its partner, and deposited the whole thing in the back of my bottom dresser drawer. After all, I might need them at the end of the year when we voted on new members for the house. If, of course, the house lasted that long.

It didn't matter how the black marbles had wound up in my possession—who might have put them in my desk. It didn't. Today was a new day. A new start. I had to focus. There was no time to dwell. No time to freak myself out.

I showered, downed some more Tylenol to take the edge off my stubbornly clinging headache, and dressed up for my first day as

Single Reed. In-Charge Reed. A Reed with a Purpose. Black skirt, black boots, light blue V-neck sweater. I was going to show the world that my breakup wasn't getting to me—even though every time I thought about it, I felt like collapsing into a heap on the floor.

At breakfast, I strolled over to my usual table with Constance, Sabine, and Kiki in tow and waited for them to settle in among the rest of the Billings Girls. Then I placed my tray at the end of the table and forced a bright smile.

"Everyone, I have an idea."

Silence fell. Kiki took the earbuds out of her ears. I noticed for the first time that her bangs were no longer pink. Instead, her blond hair was streaked with royal blue.

"Do tell," Noelle said, looking up at me as she tore off a chunk of her bagel.

"We should hold the fund-raiser in New York," I announced.

The Billings Girls murmured in excitement and tired eyes brightened all around our two tables. My heart fluttered with pride.

"Most of the Easton alumni live there or close by, so why not bring the party to the money?" I suggested.

"*Absolument!*" Sabine exclaimed. "I have always wanted to visit New York!"

"It's perfect," Tiffany chimed in.

"And we should definitely do it before Thanksgiving," I added as I took my seat across from Noelle. "Before everyone starts jetting off on their holiday vacations."

"Reed, you are so brill," Portia said with a smile.

"But that's less than three weeks," Missy, or Miss Negative, put in from behind me. All I wanted to do was turn around and yank on her braid, but it was way too kindergarten.

"We can pull it off," Noelle told her. "My mom and I organized my dad's fiftieth in less than a week. We *always* forget his birthday until the last minute," she added, rolling her eyes. "And he's such a baby if he doesn't get his party."

I smirked. I had never met Noelle's parents, but I imagined her father as a Daddy Warbucks type, all bluster and bravado. So somehow, thinking of him getting pouty over a party amused me.

"Reed Brennan," a silky male voice said at my side.

I looked up into the stunning blue eyes of Hunter Braden, the number one most sought after guy on the Easton campus. Every single girl at my table minus Noelle blushed at the very sight of him. His tousled blond hair, chiseled cheekbones, and rumpled-prep style had been splashed over all of New York's favorite rags at the end of last year when he'd briefly dated a certain hotel magnate's daughter and disappeared with her for several days to some remote island I had never heard of. Ever since, all the gossip on campus had been about whom he'd date next.

"Hunter," I replied as coolly as possible, even though I could feel my face overheating. Even my broken heart was not immune to his gorgeousness and charm. He was wearing a wrinkled Ralph Lauren oxford in light blue, with a yellow and navy striped tie casually loosened around his neck—and pulling the look off like nobody's business. Two books were hooked in his fingers at his side. No one had ever seen Hunter with anything so prosaic as a book bag.

"I want to take you out," he said with an almost irresistible smile. "This weekend."

Someone behind me literally gasped. Noelle's eyes widened across the table. I was so stunned I couldn't even speak. Then Vienna kicked my shin so hard I saw stars. Damn pointed-toe boots.

"Um." *Ow.* "That's really nice, but . . . can I let you know later?"

I feared the pain Vienna might inflict upon me if I gave him an outright no. Besides, it never hurts to play hard-to-get, right?

Hunter appeared confused. Most likely no one had ever done anything but blurt an emphatic yes to one of his offers. "Excuse me?" he said.

"Well, it's just . . ."

I just broke up with the love of my life. I wasn't sure I was ready to start dating. Especially not someone like Hunter Braden. Somehow I knew the experience of going out with him would be overwhelming even if I wasn't on the rebound.

"I have so much to do right now with the fund-raiser and everything. . . . I just have to . . . check my schedule," I rambled. "Thanks for asking, though."

I could feel the poisonous looks of every one of my friends boring into my skin from all angles. How dare I put off Hunter Braden? Hunter, however, simply smiled.

"You check that schedule of yours." He took a couple steps backward and spread his arms out at his sides as if to give me a good look at what I'd be missing if I said no. "You know where to find me."

He turned on his heel and strode off toward the Ketlar tables, the eyes of every non-geriatric female in the room trained on him. Vienna pulled back and kicked me again, right in the same spot.

"Vienna! Ow!" I said through my teeth, rubbing my leg. "Do I have to start wearing my shin guards to breakfast?"

"What the hell was that?" London demanded, tossing her fork down with a clatter.

"What? Guys, I told you. I am not ready to go out with anyone right now," I said.

"Hunter Braden is not 'anyone,'" Portia hissed, leaning across the table. "Hunter Braden is . . ." She turned her palms up and searched the skylights in the high ceiling as if God might provide a word worthy enough to describe him. "He's Hunter *Braden*."

"Exactly," Vienna said. "Besides, Reed, the best way to get over a breakup is to A, get back on the horse and B, make it a super-hot horse so that C, the last horse gets very, very jealous."

"And there is no horse hotter than Hunter," Tiffany put in from a few seats down.

Wow. Even levelheaded Tiff was behind this. Did no one understand what it was like to lose the love of your life?

"I appreciate the concern, you guys, as disturbing as the horse metaphor is," I said, spearing a strawberry with my fork. "But I'd rather focus on saving Billings. You do realize that if we don't figure out how to raise five million dollars in the next month, life as we know it is history. We're talking no more Billings, no more Friday night movies and mojitos, no more Fat Phoebe parties, no more Billings alumni–funded outings . . . nothing. We'll be living in, like, Pemberly or something."

My friends all exchanged serious glances and I knew that I had, at least for the moment, gotten their attention. For the rest of the period, we discussed ideas for the fund-raiser and I forced myself not to look over at the Ketlar table. Not to look at Josh *or* at Hunter Braden. I can't say I wasn't intrigued by Hunter's proposal. He was practically a celebrity. But he wasn't Josh. I didn't want anyone who wasn't Josh. I was still clinging to the hope that Josh might wake up one morning and forgive me. Might realize that I was beyond drunk that night and that technically I couldn't be held responsible for my actions. Just like I hadn't held him responsible for his actions with Cheyenne, because he had been drugged. Yes, I had fantasized about being with Dash before it had happened, but Josh didn't know that. Therefore, he could not hold it against me. He could, however, hold a date with Hunter Braden against me.

As we moved on to the chapel for morning services, I grabbed Rose and pulled her aside just outside the cafeteria doors. We hung back until all our housemates had strolled on, caught up in their own conversations.

"Everything okay, Reed?" she asked, ducking her head slightly so that her red curls fell forward over her cheeks. Rose was one of the more discreet girls in Billings and I knew she was intimately aware of how everything worked. At the moment she was the only person I felt comfortable asking what I had to ask. What I had been wanting to ask all through breakfast.

"Just a random question," I said under my breath. "You know all that stuff we used for the inner-circle ritual—the lantern and the . . . the marbles and everything?"

"Yeah?" Rose looked surprised.

"Where do we keep all that stuff?" I asked. "Is it in the basement somewhere, or . . ."

Rose blinked. "Actually, I think Cheyenne had all that stuff in her room. Crap, I never even thought of that. It must have gotten boxed up and sent home with her parents."

Not all of it.

I swallowed against my suddenly dry throat. Cheyenne had the black marbles? Cheyenne? Then how the hell had they gotten into my desk drawer over the weekend? Cheyenne's parents had carted away her things weeks ago. Unless someone had lifted them before then. Had someone been planning to do this all along? And if so, who?

"I guess we'll have to replace all of that before the end of the year," Rose mused with a shrug, not knowing that the info she had imparted was causing me to have major heart palpitations. "Great. Where are we supposed to find a lantern like that?"

"Not a clue," I replied.

Although maybe it would just appear in my room somewhere.

CRÈME DE LA CRÈME

After an intense soccer practice and a hot shower I was feeling almost normal. Definitely lighter. Somewhat positive, even. I could do this. I could live without Josh. Sure, the dread I had felt all day at the possibility of bumping into him around every turn had taken its toll, but the exercise and scrub-down had rejuvenated me. For the first time all day, I felt able to breathe.

As I slipped into my navy blue Easton Academy sweats and brushed my damp hair, I realized something was off. It was too quiet. Way too quiet. Normally at this time of night, London and Vienna were blasting that annoying club music they loved, Constance was in the hall blabbing to Whit on her cell, and Missy and Lorna were running in and out of their room to Portia's or the Twin Cities', slamming doors every five seconds. But right now there was nothing. Total silence.

Considering everything that had been going on lately, my pulse raced with trepidation. Anything out of the ordinary had the potential for disaster. I put my brush down on my dresser and opened the door quietly, peeking my head out. Nothing. No one. Where were they?

"Sabine? Noelle?" I called out. "Constance?"

No response. Okay. There was a logical explanation for this. Maybe they had all gone over to Coffee Carma in Mitchell Hall. Or everyone was downstairs studying. Yes. That was it. All I had to do was go downstairs and there they'd be. I crept out of my room and tiptoed down the stairs, realizing how silly I would have looked to anyone who spotted me, but there was no one there to see. Nothing but the dead silence.

I hit the floor of the lobby, saw something move out of the corner of my eye, and froze.

"Surprise!"

My heart hit my throat, but two seconds later relief washed over me. The entire population of Billings was gathered in the parlor, champagne glasses raised. Silver bowls of strawberries and trays of chocolates were laid out on every table. Fifteen faces grinned at me as I joined them.

"What's going on?" I asked.

"Reed Brennan, it's time to play Find Your Rebound!" Vienna announced, shoving a filled champagne flute into my hand.

"Find my what?" I asked.

"We couldn't think of a good name for it," Noelle said, rising gracefully from her chair at the crux of the seating U. "Basically, we are going to help you find a man to distract you in your time of need."

She lifted a hand toward the wall behind me and I turned to find that the old group shots of Billings sisters had been cleared away, replaced by three huge corkboards. On each corkboard were several glossy eight-by-ten photos of various Easton guys, and below each photo was an index card displaying the subject's vitals: name, age, class rank, hometown, net worth. The really important stuff.

"Someone absolutely perfect," Sabine added with a grin, standing next to me.

"What are you guys talking about?" I asked warily. "You're not all going to start theorizing about horses again, are you?"

Everyone laughed. Spirits were high, considering we were under such strict probation. In fact, the last thing we should have been doing right then was drinking champagne out in the open like this. If Mrs. Naylor, our housemother, found us, we were screwed.

"Naylor's out for the night," Noelle told me, noticing my wary glance over my shoulder. "Just sit and relax and have some chocolate."

She steered me around the end of the couch where Constance, Kiki, and Astrid were sitting, and deposited me in the chair she had vacated. Rose lifted a tray of chocolates and offered it to me. I took one and bit into it. Sweet caramel oozed into my mouth. This I could get used to.

"Now, here's how this is going to work," Vienna explained, walking over to the board of boys as Sabine squeezed back onto the couch. "Each one of us has selected an Easton bachelor for you to evaluate. Our goal for the evening is to rank these guys in order of desirability for you—"

"And then you can go forth and conquer!" London finished, lifting her glass to the whoops of the crowd.

I squirmed in the cushy chair. "You guys, I already told you. I'm not ready to . . . conquer anyone."

All I could think about when I looked at those photos was how many of those guys were Josh's friends—his housemates. And how he was out there on campus right now—out there somewhere hating me. The very thought sent a sliver of glass through my heart. How was I even supposed to *look* at another guy?

"Reed, come on, this is exactly the distraction you need," Sabine said earnestly, placing her glass down and scooting forward on the love seat. She grabbed my hands and champagne sloshed over the side of my flute. "You're going to save Billings for us. Let us do this for you."

I looked into her big green eyes and realized that she sincerely thought this would work. In fact, everyone there was eyeing me with hope. Aside from Missy, of course, who was inspecting her finger-nails. All they wanted to do was cheer me up. What harm could there be in humoring them? So I would let them rank these guys according to desirability. It wasn't as if I had to put said list to use.

"Okay, fine," I said finally.

"Yay!" Constance cheered, as a few people clapped in glee.

"Portia? Would you like to present your pick first?" Vienna asked, stepping aside.

Portia rose and walked over to the board, stopping in front of a photo of a smiling guy with long black hair and a big, Cheshire cat grin. Dominic Infante. He had lived next door to Thomas and Josh last year. I had the distinct recollection of seeing him in boxers one night when I walked by his room. Not a half-bad body.

"We all know who Dominic Infante is," Portia began, clasping her hands one atop the other, as if she were a professor presenting a lecture. "But few know, because of his innate modesty, that he is a direct descendant of the princes of Italy. . . ."

"Ohhh," my friends intoned as they sipped their champagne and nibbled on their strawberries.

As she continued her speech, my eyes roamed the board, curious who my other dorm mates had chosen. I spotted Hunter Braden smirking out at me. And Trey Prescott. (Josh's roommate? Seriously?) And Jason Darlington, a cute guy who was in most of my classes. Most of the elite guys of Easton were represented, and I couldn't help but feel flattered that my housemates thought me worthy of the crème de la crème. Things certainly had changed since my Glass-Licker days.

Then my eyes fell on another familiar face at the far end of the board. Marcellus "Marc-For-Short" Alberro. I blinked, surprised. Marc was cute, no doubt, but not the kind of guy I would have expected a Billings Girl to select. He was too fidgety, too garrulous, too . . . well, short. I squinted at the card beneath his sheepishly smiling face and recognized the loopy handwriting instantly. Constance. Of course. Why was I not surprised? When it came to priorities, Constance was not your average Billings Girl.

"And that accent?" Portia was saying. "*Molto* sexy!"

The girls around me all swooned and laughed knowingly, and I finally realized this might actually be fun. So I relaxed into my chair. Relaxed into the moment. Into a night without drama.

ONLY HUMAN

"Why the hell did you pick Trey?" I asked Noelle as we emerged from the breakfast line Wednesday morning. "Did you really think I could go out with Josh's roommate?"

"Of course not. That's exactly why I chose him," Noelle whispered. "I had to pick someone, but I know as well as you do that you're not ready for a relationship. So why not pick someone whom everyone would eventually have to agree was no good?"

I smiled at her. Always thinking, that Noelle.

We took seats at our table, where everyone else had already gathered, but I found that I couldn't relax. Every time the dining hall door opened, I flinched. I forced myself not to look up each time, but would glance over casually a moment later to check who had entered. If my friends had thought their game of Find Your Rebound would make me forget about Josh, they were mistaken. Of course, *they* had forgotten about him entirely. My fifteen bachelors were the number one topic of breakfast conversation.

"I can't believe you guys ranked Marc fifteenth," Constance said despondently, pushing her oatmeal around with her spoon. "I mean, you don't even know him."

"Exactly. And that's strike number one," Noelle replied. "No one here has ever talked to him but you. What does that tell you about him?" Constance's shoulders sank. She looked like a little kid who'd just been told her new puppy was hit by a car.

"I've talked to him," I said.

My words had the desired effect. Suddenly Constance sat up straight and looked at me all bright-eyed. "You have?"

"Yeah," I said with a casual shrug. "And I liked him."

"Omigod, yay!" Constance exclaimed, dropping her spoon. "So are you going to ask him out?"

"Ew! No!" Vienna exclaimed as she wrapped her thick hair back in a ponytail. Her massive breasts bulged forth from her low-cut shirt as she did so, and a freshman boy tripped himself as he walked by. Vienna didn't seem to notice. "Reed, you cannot start with what's-his-face. If you do, then last night was totally pointless."

"His name is Marc," Constance said, gaining confidence from my backup. "And he's totally sweet and the most determined reporter on the paper, and he's cute, too—*I* think."

Constance was editor-in-chief of the *Easton Chronicle* and therefore had this whole other life I knew almost nothing about, which included friendships with people like Marc.

"Good. Then you go straddle the guy," London said. She was now working on her own ponytail. Heaven forbid the Twin Cities should be seen without matching hair.

Constance blushed and fell silent again. "I don't want to straddle him," she said, making a choking noise in the back of her throat. "I have Whit."

"Good, then you go straddle *him*, and let us help Reed snag someone worthy of the Billings president," Noelle replied.

"Exactly. Just not Trey Prescott," Astrid put in.

Noelle smiled triumphantly. Her plan was working.

"Why not Trey?" London said. "He's a total hottie."

"True, but the last person he dated was Cheyenne," Astrid said, popping a grape into her mouth. "Reed's already taken over the presidency. Wouldn't dating Trey be a bit too morbid?"

For a long moment no one spoke. My heart felt sick. What was Astrid implying? That I was trying to take Cheyenne's place? I knew she and Cheyenne had been friends for years, but she had told me they were never that close. So this was an odd comment to make. Was she upset with me for taking the presidency and running with it? Upset enough, perhaps, to plant black marbles in my desk drawer?

"What?" Astrid said innocently as everyone looked at her. "I'm just saying I think people would talk."

"Okay. Moving on . . ." Noelle said, shaking her head incredulously.

"Hunter is right over there, Reed," Tiffany said, leaning in from the far end of the table. "Why don't you go talk to him?"

I glanced over at Hunter, who sat at one of the smaller tables with

Trey and West, looking as hot as ever in a striped shirt and semi-destroyed blazer. My eyes instantly flicked to Josh's usual table, but he wasn't there. Still, that feeling of longing in my heart told me all I needed to know.

"I just can't, you guys," I said. "I'm not ready to—"

The cafeteria doors opened, and this time I looked right away. The entire cafeteria seemed to screech to a standstill as Josh Hollis and Ivy Slade strode through those doors together. He was wearing my favorite sweater of his—high-collared and gray—and looked amazing, his dark blond curls all tousled by the wind. She looked like a witch in her slim black coat, her raven hair parted down the middle. A gorgeous witch, but a witch nonetheless. A witch whose head was bent so close to Josh's as they walked and whispered, I saw their temples brush. As I sat there, catatonic, the pair of them strolled right by me. Right by me without a glance.

I felt like I was going to retch. "They're not—"

I couldn't even finish the sentence.

"I don't know. They *have* been hanging out a lot the last couple of days," Missy sang, sounding happy to impart the gossip.

No. Not possible. Why Ivy? Why did it have to be Ivy? Did he hate me that much?

"Are you all right?" Sabine asked me.

"She's fine," Noelle replied for me. She leaned across the table. "What you're feeling right now, Reed? You need to use that. Get up and go over to Hunter. You don't have to marry the guy. You just have to talk to him long enough to make Josh green."

"She's right," Shelby put in, checking her brows in a compact. "God put hot boys on this earth for this very purpose."

Josh and Ivy emerged from the breakfast line together. Walked to a table together. Sat down together. Alone.

Apparently he was *not* going to wake up one day and forgive me. Was not going to realize that me hooking up with Dash while drunk was right on par with him hooking up with Cheyenne while drugged. Apparently he was just going to move on. With the girl I loathed most at Easton.

Screw him. Screw. Him.

"Fine," I said. I pushed myself up and pressed my hands into the table for a moment, steadying my knees. "I'm going."

I turned, cleared my throat, and tossed my hair over my shoulder. This gave the entire cafeteria time to take notice. To see that the Billings president was on the move. In the beginning the fact that everyone was constantly watching me had been disturbing, but today I would use it. Today everyone would be talking about how Reed Brennan made her move on Hunter Braden.

Slowly, I strolled toward Hunter's table, my heart pounding sickly in my chest. Even with all of the eyes in the room watching me, I could feel Josh's on my back.

You think Ivy hurts? Try this.

Hunter looked up as I approached. I pulled out the chair across from his and sat slowly, gracefully. Trey and West didn't seem to know what to make of me. They both just stared.

"Reed Brennan," Hunter said. Even through all the misery and posturing, it killed me the way he said my full name. So. Hot. "Knew you'd come around."

"I know a good offer when I see one," I replied smoothly.

Hunter's smile widened. West looked grim for a moment, thinking, probably, that I had blown him off because I liked Hunter, but then he and Trey started up their own private conversation. He hadn't texted me yet, as he had promised, and I supposed he wouldn't now. Oh well. I could only deal with one high-profile conquest at a time anyway.

Hunter produced his BlackBerry from his pocket. He slid it across to me, then folded his hands on the table. "Give me your digits."

I picked it up, leaning my elbows on the table so that the Black-Berry would be more visible, and slowly typed in my numbers. It was at that moment that Josh got up and stormed out of the dining hall, leaving Ivy all alone.

One gulp of guilt. Just one. That was all I allowed myself. And after that, I just felt good. Really good. Maybe it's wrong, but I did. Josh was canoodling with the enemy. And after all, I'm only human.

THREAT

That afternoon after class, I walked back to Billings to change for my final soccer game of the season, my head bent as I hungrily read *Vanity Fair*—the novel, not the magazine—which was the new assignment for English class. I had read the book before and hated it. Now I couldn't for the life of me remember why. It was a good thing that people had started to dodge out of my way wherever I went, like we all used to do as freshmen back at Croton High when the seniors appeared in the hall. Otherwise I would have been blindly mowing people over.

"Reed! Reed! Wait up!"

I ripped myself out of Becky Sharpe's world and back into my own. Students peppered the walks and the doorways of dorms, chatting before club meetings and practices and study sessions. I was halfway across the quad, between the class building and Billings, and had been about to trip over a stone bench. Good thing whoever was calling me had stopped me.

"Hey!" Jason Darlington jogged up to me, his cheeks ruddy from the cold and exertion. His shaggy, reddish-brown hair fell perfectly in place, the bangs almost covering his blue eyes. Jason was cute in that innocuous Disney Channel way. He had, in fact, been a child actor, but had never hit the big time.

"How do you walk so fast and read at the same time?" he asked with a smile.

"Special talent," I replied. "What's up? Did you miss the English assignment?"

"Nah, I was just curious why you agreed to go out with Hunter Braden," Jason said, tossing his bangs back. They fell right back into place. "You deserve better."

Okay, presumptuous. How did this guy know what I deserved? But still, I realized he was complimenting me, so I let it go.

"I mean, did you notice that the only pronoun in his vocabulary is *I*?" Jason joked.

I laughed. "He does have a bit of a self-confidence issue. In that he has too much."

"Exactly," Jason said, exhibiting some adorable dimples. "So forget about him and go out with me instead. I promise I've heard of the word *you*."

Okay, was it just me, or had three cute, popular guys just asked me out in the space of three days? Even for a Billings Girl, this was pushing it. I narrowed my eyes, recalling that Jason was number three on our eligible-bachelor list, right after Hunter and Dominic.

"Did London put you up to this?" I asked, tucking my book into my bag.

Hunter was Vienna's pick, after all. And as much as the Twin Cities loved to copy each other, they could be competitive, too. Maybe London had put Jason on my case to try to thwart Vienna and Hunter. But Jason's expression was one of total confusion.

"London? London Simmons?" he said. "I don't think I've talked to that girl since we did summer stock at that regional theater in Bucks County together three years ago."

Wait a minute. London did summer stock? Hello, left field. I never knew she was an actress. I had to file that one away for later. I eyed Jason to see if he was making this up, but he wasn't that good an actor.

"So, what do you say? You. Me. Library. Thursday night? We can study for the English exam together," Jason suggested eagerly.

I hesitated for a moment, thinking of Josh. Wondering what he would think of me if he spotted me with Hunter one day and Jason the next. But then, what did I care? Josh was done with me and had moved on to Ivy. I could do what I wanted. I was single. I was the president of Billings. And Jason was ridiculously adorable.

"Sure," I said. "I'm in."

"Great!" Jason's face lit up. "I'll meet you in the library at seven-thirty."

"Perfect."

He jogged off so jauntily I half expected him to suddenly break into song. I turned around, feeling pretty good about myself, until I found myself face-to-face with Ivy Slade.

"What do you want?" I snapped automatically.

"I just wanted to tell you it's not going to work," Ivy said, her blue eyes boring into mine. "This little fund-raiser of yours. We're all so sick of you people and your entitlement complex. Everyone at this school wants to see you fail, and we're going to make sure that you do."

My face burned. "Is that a threat?"

"It's a fact," Ivy replied with a smirk. "Even your perfect ex is with me on this one. You really destroyed him, Reed. Noelle must be so proud of her little prodigy."

I wanted to strangle her for mentioning Josh, but I somehow managed to keep my composure. I wouldn't give her the satisfaction. "What is your problem with Billings?" I demanded. "What did we ever do to you?"

Ivy turned slightly and glanced back at my dorm. Noelle, London, Vienna, Portia, and Shelby were hanging around outside, lounging on the low stone walls that led up to the door. Ivy's jaw clenched, her skin as white as ivory. For a split second, I saw so much pain in her eyes that I practically felt it. But then she turned her back on Billings and she was Ivy again. Cold, disaffected Ivy.

"Plenty," she responded, looking me dead in the eye, her expression fierce.

As she spun on her heel and stalked off, I was left wondering what, exactly, my Billings sisters might have done to inspire that kind of anger. Was it real or just something Ivy had perceived? I had no idea, but someone in that house knew. And that someone was going to spill.

BLAME GAME

It was our final soccer game of the season against Barton School, and we were deadlocked at zero. Almost ninety minutes of soccer played and nothing to show for it. As I raced up the field with the ball, all I could think about was scoring. I had to score before the whistle. I had to win. I needed this.

A cold wind whipped all stray hair back from my face toward my ponytail as I charged forward. The scrappy defender who had been giving me trouble all day raced toward me from the right. She slid for the ball, but I popped my toe under it at the last second and it sailed right over her outstretched leg. She was still ground-bound, so in the next moment I had to vault myself over her, too. Somehow I ended up on my feet with the ball, while she was still in the dirt. The crowd on the Easton sidelines—larger than normal, since it was the last game of the year, I assumed—went crazy.

"Nice move, Brennan!" someone shouted.

I just kept going.

Score. I had to score.

Ten yards from the goal. Five. The goalie was watching me like a hawk. Still, I had figured out her weakness. Too short. No wingspan. If I could kick it into the upper corner above her head, glory would be mine. I could see the shot in my mind. Could see the ball sailing past her outstretched fingers. And then, out of the corner of my eye, I glimpsed Noelle. She was open on the other side of the field. Somehow she had evaded her defender, who was now sprinting toward her from behind.

Noelle was a senior. This was her final game. And the timing was perfect. I wanted to score, but an assist would be just as good.

I glanced into the upper corner of the net where I would have kicked the ball. The goalie bought it and scooted to her right. Instead, I sent the ball zooming across to Noelle, who lobbed it easily into the net behind the goalie's back. The girl reacted, but it was far too late. By the time she dove, the ball was already hitting rope.

"Yes!" Noelle cheered

We all sprinted over to pile on her as the whistle blew. Game over. An Easton win. Noelle had gotten to score the winning goal in the final game of her prep school career. Thanks to me.

"Nice pass," she said as I clasped her hand. She gave me a knowing look, and I knew she realized what I had done for her.

"Nice goal," I replied.

As we made our way over to the stands with the rest of the team, slapping backs and smiling, I noticed for the first time that there was something off about the crowd. There were more parents in attendance than usual, there to cheer on their graduating daughters, but the rest of the crowd was made up of guys. Almost exclusively. On both sides. Not only had the Easton men come out in droves, but the Barton men were also well represented. Normally the stands were almost empty for our games, and certainly guys had never been a big contingent. What was the deal?

"Nice moves, Brennan!" one of the senior guys shouted as we all made for the water jug.

"I like a team player!" another called out to me.

At that, a couple dozen guys applauded and whistled and hooted, all directing their attention at me. Even the Barton guys were clapping for me. I caught Jason Darlington hooting in my direction with a knowing smile, as if we were sharing some private thought, though what that would be I had no idea. My skin was already red from exertion, but now an embarrassed blush fueled it further.

"Okay, what's going on?" I asked Sabine as she handed me a cup of water. Sabine had gone out for soccer at the beginning of the year, but Coach Lisick had decided that her talents were more suited for the position of team assistant. She got into the game every once in a while—it was an Easton rule that everyone got some playing time—but only when we were winning hugely or losing hugely.

"They're all here for you," she whispered to me. "They've been talking about you throughout the game."

"Seriously?" I asked, glancing around at the dozens of faces, some familiar, some not.

"That's what happens when the hottest girl at Easton suddenly hits the market," Noelle said, resting her forearm on my shoulder and leaning into me as she checked them out. "Salivating boys come from all over."

I'd had no idea it was possible to be so mortified and so flattered all at once. As I looked around, I saw random guys jostling for a better look at me. Like I was a celebrity or something. Floppy-haired boys, crew-cut boys, tall boys, short boys, cute boys, hot boys, scrawny boys, chubby boys. All of them smiling at me. Checking me out. After a few seconds I had to turn away. It was too bizarre.

"I'm gonna go . . . get some ChapStick before we shake hands," I mumbled to my friends.

I walked to the far end of the Easton bleachers, hoping to duck out of sight and dig through my soccer bag for a few moments to get a breather. As soon as I came around the side, though, I stopped in my tracks. Astrid was crouched down in the pile of duffel bags and gym bags, pawing through *my* stuff.

For a long moment, I didn't say anything. My heart all but stopped. I couldn't believe what I was seeing. Why was she going through my things? *Was* Astrid the one who had blackballed me? Was she leaving something else in my soccer bag? I thought we were friends.

I opened my mouth to speak, but at that exact moment she finally stood. There was something in her hand, but I couldn't tell what it was. She turned, saw me standing there, and nearly tripped herself. Snagged.

"You startled me!" she said with a laugh.

"What were you doing in my bag?" I demanded.

Her smile faltered, as if she was confused by my tone. "I guess you caught me," she said, flashing her palm. "I stole a barrette."

She held up her palm. One of my plain snap barrettes sat in her hand.

"Sorry. My bangs are driving me crazy," she said, flipping her short, sweaty hair back to illustrate how the bangs fell right back into her eyes. "I just wanted something to pin them for the team meeting. Is that okay?"

I glanced at the bag again, trying to decide whether to believe her. It was a simple enough explanation, but my suspicious side was on high alert these days.

"Sure," I said finally. "No problem."

Astrid smiled awkwardly and started past me.

As she walked off to join the team, I dropped onto my butt on the ground, pulling my bag into my lap. Quickly but carefully, I removed everything. My sweatshirt, my towel, my water bottle, my extra shin guards. I even opened the smaller nylon pouch where I kept my key, ChapStick, and hair bands. Everything was there except that one barrette. And there was nothing out of the ordinary. When the bag was empty, I turned it upside down and shook it, checking to see if anything would fall out.

Nothing. The bag was clean. I looked up and saw Astrid high-fiving Bernadette Baskin. Sure, Astrid had always been nice to me, a friend. But with everything that had been going on lately, I couldn't be too careful. It looked like I was just going to have to get used to being suspicious all the time. At least until I figured out who was to blame.

ENTWINED

After the soccer game, we got down to business. If we were going to throw this fund-raiser, it was time to get serious. I called a meeting for eight o'clock in the parlor and by seven fifty-five, everyone was seated on the couches and settees. Noelle sat in one of the two wing-backed chairs. I took the other. She and I had already come up with an agenda for the meeting, so I dove right in.

"First things first," I began. "We know, at the very least, that we want the event to include a dinner, so next weekend, Noelle and I will be going to New York to scout locations. London, Vienna, we're hoping you'll come with."

"Really?" London squealed.

"Road trip!" Vienna added.

They lifted their hands and slapped them together, clasping them for a moment before releasing each other.

"Why do they get to go?" Missy lamented.

Like I'd take you with me instead. I'd rather endure Chinese water torture. I'd rather be forced to watch Josh and Ivy make out for ten minutes.

Okay. Maybe not.

"Because they have the most connections," Noelle replied coolly.

"Oh, we so do," Vienna replied, laying her manicured hand out flat. "We can get all kinds of free crap from people."

"It's what we do," London confirmed. "No one can say no to us."

They looked at each other and giggled, which made all of us wonder what, exactly, they did to make themselves irresistible. But I wasn't about to ask.

"Okay, so now that that's settled, we need to make sure this is the event of the season," I said, popping the top off my pen. "It has to be original. It has to be fabulous. It's last-minute, so it has to make people want to cancel whatever other plans they might have and make this their first priority."

My friends were riveted by my speech, each sitting on the edge of her seat, fully alert. There was a palpable energy in the room. We were going to nail this. I could feel it.

"So, any ideas?" I asked, pen at the ready.

No one said a word.

"Anything. Really. We just have to get started and then the ideas will flow," I urged them.

Skittish glances abounded. It was as if they were afraid to speak. God help us.

"I have an idea!" Lorna said finally, raising her hand. Once chunky and frizzy-haired, Lorna had lost a good deal of weight since last year, thanks to joining the Easton cross-country team, and had tamed her frizz into a sleek mane. Lately she was looking healthy—almost pretty. And it all resulted in her speaking up more.

"Shoot," I told her.

"We could do an eighties theme," she announced happily.

Everyone groaned. "Lorna, this isn't a public school prom. It's a fund-raiser. For adults," Missy said with a sneer.

Lorna sank in on herself. I shot Missy an irritated glance. Maybe eighties was a horrendous idea, but why did Missy always have to be so callous to her so-called best friend?

"What ideas do you have, Missy?" I asked.

Put on the spot, Missy blanched. "Well, we could do a silent auction—"

"I'm so over those," Portia said, rolling her eyes. "What fun is an auction when you can't beat down your opposing bidder in front of everyone?"

"Besides, what would we auction?" Tiffany asked. "Ourselves?"

Strained laughter everywhere. I looked around. These were fifteen of the smartest, most accomplished, most well-traveled and well-partied girls in North America. Did they have no thoughts?

"Anyone?" I said.

"Vicars and tarts?" Astrid suggested meekly.

"Oooh! I like that!" London exclaimed.

"You would like anything with 'tarts' in the title," Shelby joked as she checked her messages. I was pretty sure she was addicted to her iPhone at this point.

"What is vicars and tarts?" Sabine asked, wrinkling her nose.

"It's a British thing," Astrid replied. "The men dress up as holy men and the women go as streetwalkers. I know it sounds mad, but the geriatrics think it's hilarious. We do them all the time back home, but it would be exotic here, I think."

"Maybe."

I didn't like it. I mean, I could see how it could be fun on some level, but I wanted the party to be sophisticated, not like a Playboy Mansion thing. Still, I wrote it down. I had to write down something. Plus I didn't want Astrid to think I was holding the fact that she'd borrowed a barrette from me against her. Which she might actually think, considering how bizarrely I had reacted at the time.

"Anyone else?"

"We could do a beach theme. Or exotic locales," Sabine suggested, sitting up straight. "Bring summer into winter. We can bring in sand and palm trees and have everyone wear summer dresses and flowers in their hair and—"

"Should we get plastic leis as well?" Shelby joked.

Sabine blushed. "Well, people are always doing Christmas in July. Why can't we do July in the winter?"

"No one's going to go for it," Noelle said, shaking her head. "What if it snows and everyone's walking around in coconut bras and sandals? We could land everyone in the hospital with pneumonia and end up getting our asses sued. No way."

Sabine shot me a look like, *I tried,* so I smiled gratefully back at her.

"At least someone's attempting to think of something," I said.

Clearly Sabine had spoken up solely to save me from the awkward silence. "Come on, you guys. Anything?"

After another thirty minutes of quiet, broken occasionally by lame ideas, I finally closed out the brainstorming portion of the meeting. It was both exhausting and depressing.

"Let's talk about some logistical stuff," I suggested. "What else do we need to do?"

"We need a guest list," Kiki announced, popping her gum.

"Right. Good. Everyone come up with at least twenty people to invite before we meet next," I said, happy to be able to assign a task that could actually be accomplished. "What else?"

"We'll need to get passes from Cromwell for next weekend," Noelle reminded me.

"Right. He's not going to like that," I said.

"Please. Once we remind him there's a cool five mil involved, he'll have no problem writing them out," Noelle replied.

"Good point," I said. "Okay, until we figure out exactly what this event is going to be, I guess there's not much else we can do. Everyone think about it and let me know if you have any huge epiphanies."

The room filled with chatter as everyone stood and gathered their things. Why they couldn't have been that talkative ten minutes ago, I had no idea. But one thing was certain—someone around here needed to have a flash of brilliance soon, or we were going to be in serious trouble. If Ivy had sat in on this meeting, she would have been happier than Vienna and London at a Calvin Klein sample sale.

Ivy. Right. Noelle was just tucking her iPhone away and getting up to go when my conversation with the witch crossed my thoughts. Noelle had been here longer than anyone—and always seemed to know what was going on with everyone around her. She had to have some kind of insight on Ivy.

"Noelle, I have a question," I said, standing.

"And I have an answer," she replied, pausing with her hand on the back of her chair.

Typical confidence. But then, she usually did have an answer.

"What is up with Ivy Slade and Billings?" I asked.

Noelle blinked. "What do you mean?"

I shoved my notebook in my bag and shouldered it, standing across the way from Noelle. "At the beginning of the year, Portia and Rose wanted to, quote, 're-extend' Ivy's invite to Billings, but Cheyenne shot the idea down. Was she supposed to be here last year?"

Noelle lifted one shoulder. "Depends on how you look at it. She was extended an invitation at the end of her sophomore year, but she opted to decline. End of story."

Opted to decline? Who the hell declined Billings?

"But that doesn't make sense," I said, crossing my arms over my chest. "Why does she hate us so much if she *decided* not to live here?"

Noelle shrugged again and came around the chair. "Sorry, Reed," she said as she reached me. "I can't say I'm intimately aware of the inner workings of Ivy Slade's brain. Thank God."

She started past me and something inside of me clicked. I knew that dismissive tone. There was something Noelle wasn't telling me. Like I wasn't worthy of knowing. I couldn't let her keep me in the dark again. Not like last year. We were equals now. It was time to remind her of that. And there were things I knew too.

"Did you know that Ivy and Cheyenne were once best friends?" I asked, turning toward the door.

Noelle stopped in her tracks. I had startled her. Ah, sweet satisfaction.

"Who told you that?" she asked, swinging her thick hair back as she turned to face me.

I shrugged. "Just something I heard."

"Well, you heard about ancient history," she replied with a condescending smirk. "Whoever your informant is, she should update her dossier."

"It's not *so* ancient, from what I understand," I replied, thinking of the photo of Ivy and Cheyenne on their first day at Easton. That was only three years ago. They had come here as best friends.

"Reed, as long as I knew those two they were like polka dots and plaid," Noelle said, taking a step toward me. "They never got along. What is your sudden obsession with Ivy Slade anyway? She eats one meal with Hollis and suddenly you're on the warpath?"

"No warpath," I replied, ignoring the pang in my chest at the mention of Ivy with Josh. "Just natural curiosity."

"Well, bag it," Noelle said. "We have more important things to focus on. Like saving your rep as Billings president. Unless you want to go down in history as the person responsible for bringing this place down."

Satisfied that she had put me in my place, Noelle turned and strode out of the room. But she hadn't put me in my place. Not by a long shot. I was more convinced than ever that Ivy's past and her current icy demeanor were somehow entwined with Billings and even more so with Cheyenne.

Standing there alone, I suddenly saw something move out of the corner of my eye. Something outside the window. Heart in my throat, I raced over and shoved the lace curtain aside. Someone was just ducking around the corner of Billings, and I could have sworn I saw a dark ponytail being tossed in the breeze. Determined to catch Ivy at her game—whatever that game was—I started toward the lobby, but then I realized I didn't have my key on me. If I went out there, I'd have to shout up at the front windows to get someone to let me back in. So instead, I took a deep breath and told myself to chill. I didn't have to chase her. I knew it was her. But what was she doing lurking around Billings after dark? Was she waiting for us all to go upstairs? And if so, why?

Whatever Noelle said, it was clear that Ivy had a major interest in Billings. And I was going to find out what it was.

DEFENSIVE

It's difficult to research a paper on World War II when your ex-boyfriend may or may not be starting up a relationship with one of the people you loathe most. The only invasion of enemy territory I could think about was Josh potentially invading Ivy's. Not a pleasant thought. After an hour and a half in front of my computer later that night, I had exactly three sentences, all of which sounded as if they could have been written by a third-grader. I kept endeavoring to focus, sit up straight, pay attention to my notes. Then five minutes later I would find myself staring out the window, thinking about the art cemetery nightmare—with Ivy playing the Cheyenne part this time—and flinch. Only then would I realize I had stopped working. Again.

I had just woken up from one such reverie when I heard Sabine let out a mournful sigh. Propped up against her pillows on her white bedspread, she lazily turned a page in her chemistry book. Then she blew out a loud breath. Clearly, something was on her mind. I closed my laptop and turned toward her in my chair. Not like I was getting anything done here anyway.

"Hey, Sabine?"

"Yeah?" she asked, eyes trained on her book.

"Everything okay?" I asked.

"I guess."

Not exactly a positive tone. She toyed with the silver ring on her left hand, turning it around and around with the pad of her thumb.

"What's the matter?" I hooked my elbow around the back of my chair.

"Nothing." Her gaze flicked in my direction. "You'll just get angry if I tell you."

She turned the page again, not fooling anyone. The girl was getting about as much work done as I was.

"Did I do something?" I asked, dreading the answer.

I knew I had been in my own, tortured little world the past couple of days, but I couldn't afford to ostracize my friends. Especially not now. These girls were all I had left.

"It's not you," she replied, laying her book aside.

Relief. I got up and walked over to sit at the foot of her bed. "So what's up? I swear I won't get mad."

Unless you're after Josh too. Then, no guarantees.

Sabine shot me a hesitant look. Then she seemed to make up her mind. She pulled her knees up and hugged them to her, resting her chin on the left one.

"It's Noelle," she said, deep resignation in her voice.

Of course. Instantly, my shoulder muscles coiled. Truth? I was sick of Sabine complaining about Noelle. She had been doing it ever since the day Noelle had returned to Easton, and it was starting to grate on my nerves. Why couldn't the two of them just get along? Or at the very least, let each other be.

"What about Noelle?" I asked, sounding defensive.

"See?" Her green eyes widened. "This is why I didn't want to tell you! You're just going to defend her."

I took a deep breath and pulled myself all the way up onto her bed, sitting with my legs curled under so I could face my roommate. Patience, Reed. This girl is one of your best friends. Don't bite her head off for having feelings.

"You're right. I'm sorry. It's just . . . you guys are my best friends. I wish you could just bury the hatchet or whatever. But if she did something, I want to know about it. So what happened?" Sabine dropped her knees down, plopped a green throw pillow onto her lap, and toyed with the chenille fringe along the edge. "I just don't understand why it's automatically assumed that *she'll* be the one to go to New York with you. It's like whatever you do, she just expects to be included."

"Well, Noelle lives in New York. She knows the place like the back of her hand. And I've been there exactly three times," I replied. "I need her there."

"But London and Vienna are going, no?" Sabine asked. "They know the city well too."

I shifted my legs into a more comfortable position. "Well, yeah . . ."

Sabine tossed the pillow aside and leaned forward. "It just felt like once again she was in charge," she told me. "She's so proprietary when it comes to everything Billings. It's like she can't accept the fact that you're the president now."

I sighed at the overplayed riff. Sabine had been telling me this for weeks. She hadn't trusted Noelle from the moment they met, and she was overly protective of me and my presidency. I knew it must have been hard for Noelle to see someone else running things around here, but she hadn't let it show. Not once. For some reason, however, Sabine couldn't recognize that.

"It doesn't matter if she accepts it or not. It's fact," I told her. "And when it comes down to it, she has way more experience planning these events than I do. I need her help if we're going to save Billings."

Sabine slumped and looked away, reaching for the pillow again. "It just . . . it would have been nice to be invited to New York," she said morosely. "I've always wanted to see it."

Instantly, a big cartoon lightbulb snapped on over my head. This wasn't about the fact that Noelle was going on my Save Billings road trip. It was about the fact that Sabine wasn't.

"You want to go?" I said, brightening. "Why didn't you just say so?"

Sabine shrugged. "Well, you and Noelle acted like it was just for you and the Twin Cities, so . . ."

"Sabine, there is no law stating that only the four of us can go. You should totally come."

"I should?" she asked, her mood doing a quick one-eighty.

"Definitely! You have an artistic eye. I'd love to have your opinion too," I told her, pushing myself up off the bed. "Besides, every Billings Girl has to see New York. It's, like, a cultural imperative."

Sabine laughed and my heart felt a lot lighter. "Are you sure Noelle won't mind?" she asked.

I paused and looked over my shoulder at her with a mischievous grin. "It doesn't really matter, does it?" I said. "It's not up to her."

PINK

Somehow, getting up the next morning was harder than it had been all week. It was like I suddenly realized that the nightmare of being without Josh was not going to end. That I was actually going to have to do this brave-face thing every day. The thought was exhausting.

But tonight was my study date with Jason. The first date of the rest of my life. I had to get up. Get psyched. Act like the girl who was super-fine with moving on. So I stripped off my covers and swung my legs out of bed, forcing myself to smile, even though Sabine was in the shower and there was no one there to see me. I could do this. I could be fun, confident Reed. I had to be.

Then I heard a loud spattering sound and glanced at the window behind my bed. It was gray outside and raindrops battered the pane. Wind whistled past, as if to hammer home the message that stepping outside today would be frigid, wet, and decidedly unfun. I groaned, shoved my feet into my slippers to protect myself from the always-

freezing wood floors, and trudged over to my closet. Forget the Single
Reed power uniform. This was a jeans-and-sweatshirt day if I had
ever seen one.

I yanked open the door and reached up to the left side of the first
shelf for the cozy Penn State sweatshirt my brother had given me last
Christmas. As my hand fell on the embroidered white letters, I froze.
Hanging at the far end of my closet, perfectly spaced on unfamiliar
wooden hangers, were three items of petal pink clothing. A cardigan.
An oxford. A short-sleeved silk blouse. Three items of pink clothing.
Not one of them mine.

Shaking, I withdrew my hand and took a step back, as if the
clothes were going to jump off their hangers and attack. Pink? I
owned nothing pink. But I knew those clothes. Would have known
them anywhere. They were Cheyenne's. Some of her favorites.

My hand shot forward and slid the closet door shut with a bang.
My heartbeat pounded in my chest, making it nearly impossible to
breathe. What were Cheyenne's clothes doing in my closet? How the
hell had they gotten there?

*Okay, Reed, think. Take a deep breath and think. Maybe they're not
Cheyenne's. Maybe they're Sabine's. She likes colorful clothing. Maybe she
hung them up in your closet by mistake.*

Feeling slightly comforted by this theory, I breathed in again and
opened the closet door. I tentatively reached for the sweater and held
it out at arm's length. Little white roses embroidered around the collar. Tiny mother-of-pearl buttons. Instantly, I was assaulted by images
of Cheyenne wearing this sweater. Laughing at some stupid joke of

Gage's in the dining hall, slipping it over her shoulders in the parlor when she got cold one Friday night last spring. It was Cheyenne's, definitely Cheyenne's.

There had to be a logical explanation for this. Maybe someone had taken these clothes from Cheyenne's room before her parents had packed it up. Maybe they had sent them out to get laundered and somehow they had ended up in here. London and Vienna had a cleaning woman come every week to work on their room. Maybe she'd been confused and had left their cleaning in my closet.

But these things hadn't been here yesterday. Had their cleaning woman, Rosaline, come yesterday? I doubted it. No, she usually came on weekends. And I was sure I hadn't heard those heavy steps of hers plodding around the hallway.

Of course, there was another, more disturbing explanation for this. Whoever had planted the black marbles in my desk drawer had planted these clothes here as well. Someone was messing with me. But why? Why would anyone want to keep reminding me of Cheyenne? Did someone know about her final e-mail? Did someone blame me for Cheyenne's death, like Cheyenne had?

Ivy. She had been skulking around Billings yesterday evening. She had claimed we had done something to her. Did she think I had driven Cheyenne to suicide? But if she was doing this to get back at me, how was she getting into Billings?

The bathroom door opened, startling me out of my skin. Sabine drew a hair pick through her long hair as she approached in her skimpy white waffle-weave robe, checking out the sweater that was clutched in my hands.

"I thought you didn't take any of Cheyenne's things after the funeral," she said, raising her eyebrows.

"So this *is* Cheyenne's," I said, my temples throbbing.

"Yes." She looked at me, confused. And why not? Shouldn't I know if I had appropriated the sweater of our dead housemate? One would think. "Remember? She spilled coffee on the cuff the morning of initiation and went into that temper." Sabine reached for the sleeve and turned it over, revealing the small, dark stain. "Why would you take a stained sweater of all things?"

"I don't . . . I didn't. . . ." Sabine's brow creased as I fought for an answer to what was, to her, a simple question. "I didn't realize it was stained."

I shoved the sweater back into the closet and slammed the door closed before Sabine could spot the rest of the pink clothing.

"Too bad." Sabine turned around and continued combing through her hair. "It was a nice sweater."

"Yeah. Nice."

I turned away from the closet. I'd wear something from my dresser instead. My fingers slipped from the knobs of the drawer as I tugged on it, slick with nervous sweat. I paused for a moment and forced myself to breathe. Sabine, meanwhile, hummed to herself as she got dressed in the far corner, oblivious to my panic.

I hadn't taken those clothes, had I? Maybe I . . . maybe I had taken them and just didn't remember. Those few days were still a blur. Everything that had gone on . . . the freaky e-mail, the funeral, the stuff with Josh . . . Maybe I had gone in there and taken some of her clothes from her room and had just blocked it out.

But this new theory did nothing to comfort me. Because if I was blocking things out, that wasn't normal. It wasn't good. If I had blocked out something that simple, what else was I not remembering? What else might I have done?

No. No. People didn't just block stuff out for no reason. They didn't just lose time unless they were on something—pills or way too much alcohol. It wasn't me. It couldn't have been me. Which left one other explanation. Someone was screwing with me. And as I yanked open my dresser drawer I resolved to figure out who it was. I was president of this house. No one messed with the president of Billings. No one messed with Reed Brennan.

Not anymore.

SUSPICIOUS BEHAVIOR

One question kept repeating itself in my mind all day. If Ivy was responsible, how was she getting into Billings? The thought of Kiki's lost key crossed my mind. Maybe Ivy had found it. Or even stolen it. If that was the case, could I get the administration to change the locks? But then I would have to tell them why. Would have to admit to potentially being stalked. And that would open up a whole can of worms I wasn't ready to deal with. Like heightened security around Billings. Like people watching me as if I was a freak. Like, possibly, explaining about Cheyenne's e-mail—explaining why Ivy or someone else might *want* to stalk me.

No, thank you. I would have to figure this one out on my own.

In the meantime, however, I had to keep up with my regularly scheduled life. And that included a study date with Jason Darlington. Fun, independent Reed was about to start her fun, independent life.

It was still raining and windy, as it had been all day long, when

I started across the dark campus, keeping to the pathways closest to the buildings in an effort to duck the weather. I huddled under my black umbrella and kept my head down as I scurried along, already looking forward to being back in my room later, cuddled up under the covers. Halfway to the library, the wind carried a voice to my ear and I looked up. Headmaster Cromwell stood just inside the open doorway of Hull Hall, shaking hands with Detective Hauer. I nearly tripped over myself when I saw them.

Detective Hauer. Lead investigator of the Thomas Pearson murder case. The man who'd arrested Josh last year right in front of me. The man who had later arrested Ariana after she tried to kill me. What the hell was he doing back on campus?

My abrupt stop caught their attention. Predictably, the Crom fixed me with a grim glare. But Detective Hauer was less in character. Last year he had almost always been nice to me—treated me as if I were his kid sister—as if he were on my side. But when he saw me there, he didn't smile or wave. Didn't even nod. He simply stared at me as if disconcerted. As if he didn't quite know what to make of me.

What was up with that?

Thrown, I quickly started walking again, and even jogged the last few steps to the library. Why had Hauer looked at me that way? And why did it make me feel so . . . guilty?

I didn't have time to dwell on it. The moment I stepped into the cozy warmth of the library, my iPhone beeped. I had a text from Jason.

u on ur way? im in 2nd flr stax. got a good corner. come up.

Study-date time. I took a deep breath, shook my damp hair back, and started up the wide staircase at the back of the marble-floored lobby. The lighting in the upstairs stacks was dim at best, provided mostly by low-wattage, fogged-glass lamps in the ceilings. Way more conducive to sleep than studying. I could hear people whispering at the ends of the packed bookshelves, ensconced in the high-backed chairs or huddled over the small tables. I even caught a telltale snore near the antiquities section. When I finally reached the end of the aisle near the window, I looked right, then left, and spotted Jason. He had not only found us a private corner, he had found us the only corner in the Easton Library with a love seat rather than single chairs. He looked up and smiled, flashing those dimples. Damn. He really was cute.

Okay, date time. If Josh could have breakfast with Ivy, then I could do this. Fun, independent Reed could do this.

"Hey," I whispered, hoping I didn't look as unattractively water-logged as I felt.

"Hey."

He was taking up one half of the small couch. I shrugged out of my wet coat and slung it over a nearby chair, out of the way. As I perched on the other side of the couch, I placed my bag on the floor and pulled out a hair band to wrap my soaked locks back in a ponytail. Once that was done I felt much more human. Much more dateworthy.

Dateworthy. I was on a date with someone who wasn't Josh. How was this possible?

"Can you believe this weather?" Jason asked. "Kinda makes you want to hunker down in here all night and wait it out."

I smiled. Way to work in the phrase "all night" before I'd even settled in. Boy was jumping right in.

"Seriously," I replied. I dug into my bag and pulled out all the novels we had read so far this year, as well as my massive notebook, all of which I dropped on the low table. "You sure you want to study here? There's not much light."

Unless you want to make out. Which is so not happening. Not even with Fun Reed. Even she isn't ready for that.

"It's fine," Jason said. "I've been here awhile. Your eyes will adjust."

His arm was draped along the back of the couch, so that when I sat down, I could feel the soft fuzziness of his sweater sleeve against my neck.

"So, what do you want to do?" I asked, restacking my books nervously. "Do you want to tackle the novels in order, or—"

"Yeah. That seems like a good plan," he replied, picking up his own, worn copy of *The Death of the Heart.*

Okay, so maybe he *was* here to study. We settled in and started to go over our notes, flipping through our marked-up, dog-eared books to remind ourselves of specific references. Jason turned out to be smart for a child star—a very perceptive reader—and before long I found myself enjoying our heated discussions.

"Wait, so you actually liked this book?" I asked, holding up my copy of *Sister Carrie* between my thumb and forefinger like it was a bag of smelly garbage.

"Okay, I admit it was *somewhat* over the top," Jason said, flashing those dimples of his as he drew his knee up on the couch to better face me. "But Dreiser had his reasons for—"

"Somewhat? Somewhat? Are you kidding me?" I demanded, my voice going shrill as I laughed. "There were points when I actually wanted to track down Dreiser's grave, dig his ass up, and beat on his bones just for torturing me."

"Um, don't you think it would be easier to take out your wrath on Winslow?" Jason suggested, his eyes sparkling. "He did assign the book."

"Point taken," I replied with a smile. "But he *is* giving me an A so far this term, so—"

"All right, then. Dreiser's bones it is," Jason joked.

"Thank you," I said, dropping the book on the table.

"You're welcome." He righted himself on the couch so that we were both facing forward again. We were both still smiling, and there was this warm camaraderie between us. A nice, friendly warmth.

"This is fun," I said.

"You sound surprised," Jason replied.

"Do I?" I said, embarrassed. "Sorry."

"It's okay."

Out of nowhere his hand fell on my shoulder. He was much closer than he'd been ten seconds ago.

"The library's gonna close in half an hour," he said, looking into my eyes.

"So?" I said stupidly.

"Sooooo . . ."

He leaned in and kissed me. I was so taken aback that I didn't even have time to stop him or pull away, and suddenly I was leaning backward, with him bearing down on me, the arm of the couch pressed into the center of my back.

Okay. Cute boy kissing you. Nice, cute boy kissing you. Don't freak out. Just . . . kiss him back. That's what Fun Reed would do.

So I tried. I tried to kiss him back. But then his unfamiliar tongue shot into my mouth and I thought of Josh. How very not-Josh this guy was. Suddenly I wanted to hurl.

"Jason, stop," I said, pushing him gently away and sitting up. Maybe there was still a way to salvage this. Get out of this gracefully and retain Jason as a friend. It wasn't his fault I was on the rebound, after all. He was just doing what half the other guys at this school seemed to want to do—land the Billings president. "I can't do this right now," I said.

"Sorry. Sorry," he said awkwardly, tugging at his pants legs as if to de-wrinkle them. "I'm such an idiot."

"No. It's okay. It's just—"

"You're not over Hollis yet. I get it." He was all red as he flashed me a self-deprecating smile. "I just figured that since he was already hooking up with Ivy Slade, you might be ready to, you know—"

My heart plummeted. "What?"

"What what?" Jason asked, surprised by my outburst.

"Who told you they hooked up? Did he tell you that?" I asked.

"No! I—"

"Then who told you?" I demanded.

"No one. Someone," Jason babbled. "I don't know! Everyone's talking about it."

Everyone's talking about it. Everyone but the people around me. If there was something going on, the Billings Girls knew about it. What were they trying to do, protect me?

"I have to go to the bathroom," I said, feeling more nauseated than ever. I had to get out of there. I had to think.

"Wait! Reed, are you okay?"

"I'm fine," I mumbled. "I'll be back."

Then I turned and fled. Ivy and Josh, Ivy and Josh, Ivy and Josh. Suddenly the images my mind had conjured the night before took on a new and realistic clarity. His hands in her thick black hair, her short-but-toned legs wrapped around him. I had to cover my mouth to keep from throwing up as I raced down the staircase toward the bathrooms on the first floor.

Please don't let me boot in the middle of the library. That's the last thing I need.

At the bottom of the staircase I was about to turn toward the bathrooms when I saw him. Josh himself. He had just walked in through the front door and now stood, his curls glistening with rain, directly across from me. The length of the lobby separated us, the low glass cases displaying Easton artifacts acting as a barrier. But we might as well have been face-to-face. For a long second neither of us moved. Time stopped.

How could you? How could you hook up with someone just days after we broke up? Did I mean nothing to you?

You hooked up with Dash before *we broke up,* Josh's voice replied in my mind. *And don't even try the "I thought you dumped me" line. Even if I had, what you did was still horrible.*

Silent conversation over, Josh turned and walked toward the circulation desk, which was hidden from my view by the floor-to-ceiling bookshelves. I forced myself to make a left and walk to the bathroom alcove, but before I went inside, I glanced down an aisle between the stacks. Glanced at the tall oak desk. Josh stood there with Ivy, her head tipped sideways against his arm in a comfortable way, as if they had been dating for years.

That was it. That was all I needed to see. From here on in, Josh Hollis was nothing to me. I would date every drop-dead-gorgeous guy at this school if that was what it took to get over him, and he would just have to watch it happen.

From now on, Reed Brennan was on a mission. Forget the bathroom. I turned on my heel and walked determinedly back upstairs to Jason. Back to my date. Back to my new life.

PRESIDENTIAL

"You do realize we're not going to New York until *next* weekend," I said to Sabine on Friday night. Her bed was covered with clothing, sorted by skirts, tops, pants, sweaters, and miscellaneous accessories, and she was systematically removing everything from her closet to add to the piles.

"I know. I just want to make sure there's nothing else I need," Sabine replied, studying a long-sleeved azure dress. "If *Maman* is to send something from home, I have to tell her tomorrow or it won't get here in time."

Sabine wanted to look stylish for our trip to the city. Which I understood. It was the cool capital of the world. But I had enough trouble looking of-the-moment at Easton. Trying to do the same in New York would probably make my head explode.

She took the last few things out of her closet and closed the door with a bang, which forced the door of my closet to pull back an inch.

My heart caught in my throat. I hadn't been in my closet since yesterday morning, which meant that today I had worn the same jeans and shoes as I had yesterday. So far, my fashionista friends either had not noticed or had refrained from saying anything, but that wouldn't last long. Tomorrow I'd have to venture into my wardrobe again, but for now, I got up and closed the door without so much as a peek inside.

I didn't want to think about those clothes. Didn't want to think about what they meant. Avoidance was key to sanity.

"Everybody decent?" Noelle asked, striding right into our room without waiting for the answer.

She dropped down on the edge of my bed, leaning back on her hands and kicking her legs out, crossing them at the ankle. She was wearing camel-colored suede ankle boots with little silver buckles across the backs. Here was a girl who hadn't worn the same shoes twice since she'd arrived on campus a month ago.

"So, the good news is, Dash is going to be in the city next week too," Noelle announced.

My heart leapt through my back into my bra strap, then slingshot its way through my body into my ribs. Dash was going to be there. Dash still existed. I'd been starting to wonder, considering he had yet to respond to my e-mail. I guess talking to his current girlfriend was more important than explaining himself to the girl he'd totally led on. For some reason, the thought of Noelle and Dash whispering sweet nothings to each other over the phone as if he and I had never happened made my fists clench.

It wasn't that I wanted Dash. Not anymore. Especially not now that he had sat on my message for so long and hadn't bothered to call or write back. I had been enthralled by him, sure. I could admit that to myself. But that was all. And all before I realized exactly how much Josh meant to me. As for the pinch of anger, it was just that once again Noelle had won. She always, always won.

"The bad news is he wants me to have dinner with Charles and Fiona," she said, rolling her eyes. "I would never force him to have a meal with Wallace and Claire. Mostly because my mother would probably come on to him after three glasses of pinot, but still. Ugh. Now I'm going to have to be all . . . polite."

"I'm confused. Who are Charles and Fiona?" Sabine asked, neatly folding a cream-colored sweater.

"Dash's parents," Noelle said in a snotty tone, as if Sabine should have known that from birth. "The McCaffertys?" She watched Sabine with narrowed eyes as Sabine picked up another sweater and refolded it neatly. "What's up, Frenchie? Are you dropping out? Hopping a Cessna back to island paradise?"

Sabine blushed at Noelle's obviously hopeful tone.

"No. She's deciding what to bring to New York next weekend," I told Noelle, crossing over to my desk. I picked up my phone to check for messages, but there was nothing. Not from Josh. Not from Dash. "Sabine is coming with us."

Noelle laughed as she pushed herself up from the bed, lifting her heavy hair over her shoulder. "Uh, no."

Sabine shot me an alarmed glance.

"Uh, yeah," I replied, matching Noelle's tone.

Noelle looked at me, incredulous. "Reed, it's going to be hard enough to get Cromwell to give us four passes. There's just no way."

My blood started to boil in my veins. Why did Noelle always have to be so bossy? Couldn't she let me make one decision without trying to override it?

"If we can get him to give us four, we can get him to give us five," I said coolly but firmly. "I invited Sabine, and she's coming."

My tongue wanted to add an "Is that okay with you?" out of habit, but I didn't let it. Instead I bit down on it until I tasted blood. Noelle glared at me, as if waiting for me to crack, but I didn't. I simply stared back.

"Fine, Madame President," she said finally. Then she turned to Sabine. "Just don't get your hopes up. I wouldn't want you to be crushed when the Crom says no," she said in an overly sweet tone. Then she shot me a smile before turning and striding out.

"Do you really think he'll say no?" Sabine asked me, her voice hushed. She had a light blue T-shirt clutched in her hands like it was a lifeline.

"No. I'll take care of it," I said, my voice solid even though my body was quaking from the effort of standing up to Noelle. I could talk a big game, but it wasn't easy. Noelle was still the girl who had intimidated me all last fall and kept me guessing as to where I stood every single day. I had a feeling contradicting her would never be easy.

My iPhone sang out and my heart leapt. It always leapt at the sound of the phone these days, as if it was expecting Josh. Each ring was a chance that he was calling to make up. But when I grabbed the phone, it wasn't Josh's photo smiling out at me, it was Hunter Braden's. How had that even gotten in there? I could only imagine that Vienna or Portia or someone had swiped my phone and captured the pic when I wasn't looking. I took a deep breath and picked up.

"Hello?"

"Reed Brennan."

The way he said my name made my already weakened knees useless. I sat down on my desk chair. How did he have this kind of power over girls? Was that kind of talent learned or bred? I wasn't even sure if I liked the guy in a casual sense, but that voice. Incredible.

"Hi, Hunter."

"You. Me. Dinner tomorrow night. I'll come by Billings at seven."

There was something about his bold self-confidence that left a sour taste in my mouth, but I figured he couldn't keep that up all the time. Somewhere under all that product and naturally won tan there had to be a real person. Plus, Vienna and the others were right: Hunter was the perfect candidate for the Billings president's boyfriend. A smooth, sophisticated, popular, rich, Dash McCafferty type. Only better. Because he wasn't currently dating one of my best friends.

In the end, I'd had a great time with Jason—after we'd gotten over the awkward-kiss thing and decided to just be friends. Why not give Hunter a shot as well? He was the perfect guy to help me show the world exactly how over Josh I was. I could move on, too. I could move on with the best of them.

"I'm in," I told him.

"Of course you are," he replied. "See you then."

I turned the phone off but called up his picture again and considered it. A date with Hunter Braden. I was feeling more presidential by the second.

When I told Vienna that I had agreed to a date with Hunter Braden, she let out an ear-piercing shriek that definitely broke a few pairs of glasses all over campus. She spread the news quickly, and suddenly it was as if a housewide holiday had been declared. Plans were dropped. Club meetings skipped. Facials eschewed. By one o'clock on Saturday afternoon, every Billings Girl had descended upon my room, offering up color palette suggestions, wardrobe items, and some seriously dubious etiquette pointers.

"If you happen to get something caught in your throat, do not choke at the table," Shelby told me as she laid out her collection of cocktail dresses on Sabine's bed. "There is nothing less attractive than bug eyes and bread crumbs flying everywhere with your spittle."

I stopped blowing on my freshly manicured nails, which Constance and Kiki had just clipped, buffed, and polished. She had to be kidding.

"She's right. Choking will totally turn a Hunter Braden off," Portia added, organizing several eye shadow palettes on my desk for Noelle to inspect. "It is T.V."

I glanced at Rose for clarification. She was always translating for Portia. "Totally verboten," Rose explained as she sifted through her own jewelry collection for something to lend me.

"You guys are too funny." I laughed, shaking my head as I got up from Sabine's desk chair. Everyone looked at me like I was crazy.

"This is serious, Reed," Vienna said, placing both hands on my shoulders as Kiki and Tiffany tested perfumes on each other. "If it happens, get up and walk over to the bathroom and get one of the waiters to Heimlich you in private. You'll thank us later."

"Right. Unless I'm dead," I replied.

That comment killed the chatter for a moment and I froze. But it only lasted a moment. When the Billings Girls were in a makeover zone, almost nothing could stop them.

"Okay. What are we thinking for our color scheme?" Astrid asked, holding a black silk dress under my chin, then a shimmery blue sheath.

"Watch her nails!" Lorna gasped

She and Missy—yes, even Missy was there—jumped up and held my arms out at my sides like a *T* so that Astrid could continue testing clothes under my face without messing up my manicure. I was starting to feel like a rag doll.

"I still say red," Tiffany put in, stepping up to study me over Astrid's shoulder. "Red is her color."

"I think pink," Shelby said, sitting on the foot of my bed. "Why don't you ever wear pink, Reed. Don't you own anything pink?"

My heart stopped beating. I looked at Shelby. Did she know something? Had she done something? Was that a teasing smirk in her eyes? Or was I just completely and utterly paranoid?

"Actually, she does have pink!" Sabine announced, bounding over to my closet. "What about that—"

"No!"

My mouth was open, but I hadn't said anything. It was Noelle who had spoken and commanded the attention of the room. Sabine stopped in her tracks.

"Pink? Did you all let your *Vogue* subscriptions lapse? Pink is so last season and *so* not Reed," Noelle said, dropping the eyelash curler she was toying with and walking over to stand next to me. "You girls can let her go now," she told Missy and Lorna. Which they promptly did. "Look at her, ladies," Noelle said. "She is no spring."

"She's right. You're a total autumn," London said seriously. Then her eyes lit up. "I know! Wear your Nicole Miller!"

"You have a Nicole Miller?" Noelle said, eyeing me with surprise.

"Yes!" I went over to my closet and whipped the dress out, tags and all, before anyone could see that the pink clothing hanging inside had once belonged to Cheyenne. I held it up for all to see.

"Not bad," Noelle said, fingering the slippery fabric.

"I bought it for her," Portia offered, happily raising her hand. She had bought it for me on the day I had been elected president of Billings. Back when I had been planning a Halloween ball in honor of

Cheyenne. Before Noelle's return and the Legacy debacle and the ten million other things that had changed in the meantime.

"Ladies, I think we have the dress!" Noelle announced. "Now, who has shoes? Because I really don't think Chuck T.'s are going to work."

Everyone giggled and dove into their shoe boxes. Suddenly pairs of peep-toes and pumps and stilettos and kitten heels were whipped at me from every direction. Noelle shook her head at some, wrinkled her nose at others, and finally settled on a pair of Tiffany's Jimmy Choos. Black with delicate straps. In about two seconds I was zipped up, strapped in, and whisked off to makeup with Astrid and the Twin Cities. Just before the bathroom door shut, I glanced back at Shelby to see if she was still watching me. See if she was gauging my reaction to her pink comment. But she had simply kicked back on my bed to check her messages, eyes glued to her phone as always.

It was just a coincidence. Had to be. Shelby Wordsworth had no reason to hate me. To torture me. Right?

ATTACK

"I can't believe this restaurant doesn't have a valet," Hunter said as he parallel parked his gorgeous Bentley on a side street in the town of Easton. A couple inches of snow had fallen earlier that day, which made it harder to see the lines, and I felt for him. Parallel parking was so stressful. Doing it on a first date couldn't be easy. "But it shouldn't be too far to walk."

"Believe me, I don't mind," I told him.

Where I came from a fancy dinner out meant not wearing jeans to the Steak & Ale. Yet here I was, decked out in thousands of dollars' worth of couture, with a guy wearing a cashmere coat and leather gloves, looking like a movie star behind the wheel. Walking a couple blocks to the restaurant was not going to kill me.

"No, no. I'll get that," Hunter said, stopping me as I reached for the car door.

I giggled to myself as he got out, strolled around the front of the car, and opened my door for me. Noelle said it all the time and I was starting to agree with her—there was no substitute for good breeding. He offered his hand, which I took—as awkward as it felt—and helped me out of the car.

"This is my favorite restaurant in town. It's not easy to get a reservation here, but they always save a table for me," Hunter said as he used his remote to lock his car.

"Must be nice," I said as we turned up the sidewalk.

"It is," he replied with a smile.

We walked carefully, avoiding patches of ice on the freshly shoveled walkway. I felt like I should be making conversation, but I was at a loss for the moment. The silence was just starting to feel awkward when we came around the corner onto Main Street and half a dozen flashbulbs flashed across the street.

"Oh, you have to be kidding me," Hunter groused.

He ducked into the doorway of a children's clothing boutique, which had already closed down for the night, and pressed his back to the brick wall.

"What? What's going on?" I asked, looking up.

"Get in here!" he hissed.

I did as I was told, hopping up the one step and huddling next to him. "What is it?" I asked.

"Paparazzi," Hunter said through his teeth. "Crap. Someone must have tipped them off that I was going out tonight. You date one social- ite . . ."

"Seriously? You're actually being stalked by the paparazzi?" I asked.

"Must be a slow news week for them to come all the way up to Connecticut," Hunter said, then cursed under his breath. "My dad warned me about this. He said they were going to want to get pictures of whoever I dated after the heiress."

"Which would be me," I said, trying to make this sink in.

"Which would be you," Hunter agreed. "Are they coming over here?"

Okay. This was surreal. I was being stalked by the paparazzi on a date. If the shallow chicks back home could see me now. Well, maybe they would when they opened next week's *Us Weekly*. Weird.

"Reed! Are they coming over here?" Hunter sounded desperate.

I peeked around the corner. The four photogs were still hanging out across the street, probably waiting for our next move. "They look like they're staying put."

"Yeah, until I come out. I'm going to kill whoever did this," Hunter said.

"Well, why don't we get rid of them?" I asked.

Hunter scoffed. "No offense, Reed, but how? You have no idea what kind of people you're dealing with."

I glanced down at the pile of snow that had been shoveled up against the wall of the shop. The idea was so basic, but so deliciously evil at the same time. "Maybe not. But I do know that no one likes a face full of icy snowball. Also, water is really bad for cameras."

Hunter followed my gaze and smiled wickedly. "I like the way you think."

I crouched to the ground in the black designer coat I had borrowed from Shelby, and Hunter followed my lead. Together we dragged as much snow into our little alcove as possible, remaining hidden from the photographers, thanks to the cars and SUVs parked all up and down the street. Quickly, silently, we cobbled together as many snowballs as we could. When we'd used up all the snow, I gathered a few balls in my arms and stood, pressing back against the wall again.

"What's the plan?" Hunter asked, his eyes full of mischief.

"We fire at will until there's no ammo left, then make a break for the restaurant. Hopefully they'll be too disoriented to follow," I whispered.

"I like it," Hunter said.

I felt a flutter of pride in my chest. Hunter Braden liked my idea.

"On the count of three," I directed. "One, two, three. Fire!"

Together the two of us jumped out of our hiding space and launched our snowballs. My first hit one of the cameras right in the lens, splattering all over its owner's face. Hunter didn't quite have my arm, but he managed to bean a couple of guys in the shoulder before we reloaded. There were a few desperate camera flashes while we grabbed more snowballs, but when we came up again, we managed to smack two more guys directly in their faces. The cursing and sputtering across the way was utterly ridiculous, and Hunter and I laughed the entire time.

"I'm out! Let's go!" Hunter shouted, grabbing my hand.

We raced up the sidewalk, me teetering in my high heels, Hunter leading the way through klatches of moviegoers and couples walking off their dinners. Before long he was opening the door of the restaurant for me, and with a glance over my shoulder I saw that none of the photographers had followed. Our assault had done the trick.

"That was intense," Hunter said, catching his breath just inside the door. He looked gorgeous, all ruffled and ruddy-cheeked from the cold. So gorgeous I almost felt unworthy in his presence.

"That may have been the most fun I've had all week," I replied with a grin.

Hunter shrugged out of his coat and looked me up and down with a new admiration in his eyes. "And we're just getting started."

Okay. This was going to be the best date ever.

NOT MY NIGHT

Or not. After five minutes alone at the table with Hunter Braden, I couldn't for the life of me figure out how anyone had ever lasted more than five minutes alone at a table with Hunter Braden. Every other sentence out of his mouth started with the word *I*. He couldn't go for more than ten seconds without talking about himself, so if I was in the middle of a sentence, and more than ten seconds had gone by, he would interrupt me mid-syllable to tell me something super fascinating and totally out of context about him, like how he'd gone deep-sea diving last summer or how he'd beaten the world chess champion when he was fifteen.

But of course, no one knew about that, because Hunter didn't want to ruin the guy's life. Plus, he wasn't one to brag.

Yeah, right.

At least he was nice to look at. In a perfectly cut dark blue suit and striped tie, he looked completely at ease and comfortable, like he'd been born in formal wear. I was feeling quite sophisticated and sexy as well, in all my couture. Not that Hunter had said a word about it or even appeared to notice. He did, however, check himself out in every reflective surface available, including the weathered silver platter that hung on the wall next to our table. No surprise, he always appeared pleased by his own reflection.

I had thought he was so cool when he'd gone for the snow war idea. But clearly that had just been a means to an end to him. I had helped him stay out of the tabloids for another day. And come to think of it, he hadn't even thanked me for it.

The restaurant was a tiny French bistro with only six tables and twice as many waiters. I tried to orchestrate a short evening by skipping the appetizers and going straight for the entrée, but Hunter—shockingly—didn't take my cue. He ordered a salad and an appetizer, then sat there and ate it in front of me while my stomach growled audibly and I sipped my ice water.

I was going to have to kill Vienna later. Or, possibly, eat her.

"So I'm definitely getting into Columbia early admission and my father has already put the down payment on the apartment I picked out," Hunter said as he nibbled on his foie gras. "We start renovations over Christmas break, so it should be exactly the way I want it by fall."

"Columbia. That's great," I said, taking a stab at enthusiasm. "How's the campus? I've always wanted to check it out."

"Who cares? It's the only Ivy in New York," Hunter replied with a shrug. He looked up and snapped his fingers, signaling a waiter to refill his wineglass. "There's no point in even looking at the others. I have to be in New York."

Oookay. "Speaking of New York, I'm going down there next weekend," I said, attempting to turn the conversation toward myself for a moment. "We're going to hold the fund-raiser there."

"What fund-raiser?" he asked, taking a sip of his wine.

"The Billings fund-raiser," I said, surprised. The whole Billings scandal had been all anyone could talk about for the past week. "You know . . . how Headmaster Cromwell challenged us to raise five million dollars to save the—"

"Five million dollars," Hunter scoffed. "My apartment will be worth more than that once I'm done with the overhaul."

My jaw clenched and I found myself clutching my tiny purse under the table. God, I missed Josh. Even though he hated Billings, he would have at least listened to me. If we were still together, he'd be supporting me right now, helping me with ideas, at least letting me finish a damn sentence. What I wouldn't give to go back in time and give pre-Legacy Reed a good slap across the face. If only I could tell her to take Josh up on his offer in the woods and just stay home that night. If only I could tell her not to go up to the roof at the Legacy. If only I could impress upon her what a nightmare that whole party would be. . . .

No. I was not going to think about that. I was supposed to be on a mission here. Creating a new Reed. Unfortunately, I was starting to think that the new Reed was too good for the current Hunter.

"I'm definitely going to create my own major," Hunter was saying.

"Something not boring. Like water-sports marketing. I could definitely be a pioneer there. I know I—"

That was it. I couldn't take it anymore. If I heard the word *I* one more time, I was going to break something.

"You really like talking about yourself, don't you?" I said.

Hunter paused, looking at me across the table with interest for the first time all evening. For a moment I thought he was going to backtrack, to apologize, to ask me something about me. But then, he smirked, wiped his mouth with his linen napkin, and leaned his wrists on the table.

"If you were me, wouldn't you?"

That was when I got up and walked out. I snagged my coat from the coat-check girl, told her to get her tip from the jackass with the permanent smirk, and headed into the cold night.

As soon as I was outside on the quaint Easton sidewalk, I tipped my head back and let out a groan, watching the cloud of steam from my breath disappear against the stars. I glanced around for lurking photographers, thinking I might tell them exactly where Hunter was and that I had just ditched him, but they were nowhere to be found. Oh, well. One thing was clear, however—it was time to take the search for the next boyfriend of the Billings president in a new direction. This particular president was not a Hunter Braden type of girl. I shoved my hands in my pockets and started walking through town toward school. It was a long trek, but that was fine by me. It was a clear, cool night and I wanted to delay my return to my room anyway. With nothing better to do, I knew I'd start obsessing about the black marbles and the pink clothing and who might have thought it would be fun to freak me out. All things I didn't want to consider.

It occurred to me somewhere in the middle of block two that Hunter might come looking for me in his Bentley, but I doubted it. He probably had yet to notice I was gone. And if he had, I was sure he didn't care.

At the edge of town I spotted the old-fashioned light posts with their big, round lamps that marked off the front of the Easton police station. Not my favorite place in the world. I approached it, my heart starting to beat erratically as I remembered the last time I had been there, the awful things that had occurred. I ducked my head and speed-walked past, feeling conspicuous. I wondered if Detective Hauer was inside. Wondered what that look had been about on Thursday night. My heartbeat didn't return to normal until I was well past the bright lights of the building and had turned onto the relatively dark Hamilton Parkway, which would take me back to the Easton Academy gate.

I kept a good distance into the shoulder, knowing I was barely visible to motorists in my black coat. Cars whizzed by, tossing my hair into my face with their back drafts. The speed limit on Hamilton was forty-five, but people routinely broke it. I was just starting to wonder if this walk was the worst idea ever when a slow-moving car approached me from behind. I turned around, expecting to see Hunter and his newly discovered conscience, but instead of the Bentley, I found myself staring into the headlights of a modest, late-model Ford. The car pulled up alongside me and Detective Hauer leaned away from the steering wheel toward the passenger-side window.

You have to be kidding me.

"Need a ride?" he asked.

"No. Thanks. I'm fine."

I started walking again, shakily. He inched forward.

"I think you need a ride," he said.

"No, really. I'm—"

"Reed, there's something I need to talk to you about." He reached over and popped the door open so that it almost hit me in the legs. "Get in the car."

A CHAT

I sat stiffly in the cold, hard chair, my bag placed on the cracked wooden table in front of me. My coat was still on. It felt colder in the interrogation room than it was outside. And besides, I wasn't planning on being here long. No need to get comfortable.

Detective Hauer walked in through the door behind me, but didn't shut it. He took a seat opposite me, placed a thick brown folder on the table, and folded his beefy hands on top of it. As unkempt as ever, he wore a green sweater with some kind of food stain near the hem, and one point of his white shirt collar stuck out while the other was still tucked in. His brown eyes looked heavier than I remembered. Behind me, the station was fairly quiet, aside from the occasional ringing phone. Nothing like the last time I was here, with the police force bustling around, trying to handle Thomas's murder and failing miserably, routinely arresting the wrong people. Including Josh.

"Don't you need my parents here or, like, someone from school if you're going to interrogate me?" I asked, wanting to show him how very un-intimidated I was, even though I was shaking in my borrowed-from-Tiffany Jimmy Choos. "I am a minor, you know."

His bushy eyebrows shot up. "I'm not going to interrogate you. I'm just on a fact-finding mission. I want to chat."

"About what?" I spat.

"Cheyenne Martin."

If I was shaking before, I was trembling now. What could he possibly want to ask me about Cheyenne after all this time? She had been dead for more than a month.

"I understand that you and Cheyenne had quite the contentious relationship," he began.

My heart was in my throat. "So?"

He blew out a sigh and leaned back in his chair, adjusting his semi-twisted sweater over his belly before lacing his fingers together over its widest point.

"Reed, I'm going to be straight with you here," he said. "Cheyenne's parents have had some time to go through her things, and they've asked us to look into the possibility that Cheyenne's death was not a suicide."

All the oxygen was sucked right out of the room with those few words. Was not a suicide. Was, therefore, a murder. I knew they had checked into this in the very beginning, but I thought they had come up with nothing. They had cremated Cheyenne's body, for God's sake—the most important piece of evidence according to any of the ten billion police procedural dramas on TV. How could they even begin to investigate something like this now?

"So you think Cheyenne was murdered," I heard myself say.

"Personally? No," he replied, sitting forward. "But I believe we owe it to the family to check out every lead."

Okay. Okay. So he *didn't* think it was a murder. Only her parents did. That was better, right? If the detective was unconvinced?

Hauer flipped open his folder and slid a piece of paper toward him. "That said, I wanted to talk to you in particular because we've just finished going through Cheyenne's computer files."

Oh, shit. Oh, crap; oh, crap; oh, crap. The room was no longer cold. Quite the opposite, actually. Was that the devil breathing down my neck?

"And we found something interesting in her e-mail outbox," he said, looking over the top of the page. "Any idea what that might be?"

He had the e-mail. He knew. He knew that Cheyenne had blamed me for her death. My worst nightmare was coming true, right here and right now. Under the table, my hands gripped the wool of Shelby's coat and my feet slipped out of Tiffany's shoes, too wet to hold them on any longer.

"Do I need a lawyer?" I asked,

Up went the eyebrows again. "Do you feel you need one?"

"I didn't do anything, if that's what you mean," I replied quickly.

"Okay then." He placed the page on the table, turned it to face me, and slid it across with his fingertips. "Why don't you tell me what this is all about?"

It was a printout of the e-mail. Her address, my address, the time sent, the subject line empty. Then the lines that had become so excruciatingly familiar over the past few weeks.

Ignore the note. You did this to me. You ruined my life.

My empty stomach clenched at the sight of them and a dry heave rose up in my throat. But I swallowed it back. As terrified as I felt—what did Hauer *think* this meant?—I also felt a slight sense of relief. Someone else had read the e-mail. It was real. It was right in front of us. Both of us. Part of me had started to wonder if I had imagined all the Cheyenne-related oddity that had been swirling around me lately. But not this. This was real. I wasn't going insane.

I took a deep breath and released Shelby's coat from my sweaty palms. "You already know Cheyenne and I were fighting." I knew this because my friends had told me the cops had been asking about us when I'd returned from a weekend in New York with Josh. They had told me that the cops knew about Cheyenne's and my screaming argument over Josh. "I got this the day after she died."

"Why didn't you report it?" Detective Hauer asked, sitting up straight again.

"I didn't think it was important," I replied automatically.

He gave me an incredulous look. "A girl blames you for her death and you don't think it's important?"

"No! Not like that," I blurted, suddenly frustrated. "Obviously I think it's important. It's practically all I think about, that she might have killed herself over something she thought I'd done to her. I mean, I don't know if she blamed me because she wanted my boyfriend and she couldn't have him, or if she blamed me because she thinks I somehow got her expelled or what, and I'm never going to know. And believe me, that *is* important to me. But is it really important to you? I mean, doesn't this e-mail sort of prove that she killed herself?" I asked, holding it up. "This was just her last-ditch effort to get to me."

"Actually, I do think this is our best piece of evidence *for* suicide," Hauer said. "I just wanted to hear what you had to say about it."

I took a deep breath. It felt good to have this out there. To have someone listen. Even if it was Detective Hauer.

"I wasn't Cheyenne's biggest fan and she wasn't mine," I said, placing the page down again, feeling a bit more in control. "But I'm sorry she's dead, and I had nothing to do with it."

The detective picked up the e-mail printout and placed it atop the other pages in his folder. "All right then," he said. "There's just one other question I have to ask. Do you know if Cheyenne had any other enemies at school? Anyone else who could help shed some light on what might have been going on in Ms. Martin's mind?" Instantly, a name popped up in my mind. A knowing smirk. Cold blue eyes. The eyes of someone who had known Cheyenne but had grown to hate her.

"What is it?" Detective Hauer asked, clearly noting the change in me—the realization in my eyes.

"Ivy Slade," I said, a bit too loudly. "You definitely want to talk to her."

I speed-walked back to Billings after Hauer dropped me off on the circle, hoping that no freshmen or sophomores with big mouths saw me getting out of the detective's car from their windows in Bradwell. If they did, the news would certainly be all over campus in the morning—Billings president leaves campus with Hunter Braden, returns with police—and that could not happen. No one was going to know about my meeting with Hauer. No one was going to know that Cheyenne's parents had asked the police to open up a murder investigation. Not if I could help it.

I remembered all too vividly the dreary, morbid, terrified atmosphere on campus once it was revealed that Thomas had been murdered. I couldn't go through that again. This school couldn't go through that again. Especially considering there was still a good chance Cheyenne had taken her own life. I mean, if she hadn't, then why had I gotten her suicide note? It made no sense. I wished Hauer had told me what kind of evidence her parents had discovered that had spurred them to reopen the case. I couldn't imagine what it could possibly be. The girl had been found alone on her floor with pills and a note. No signs of a struggle. No one in the dorm had heard a scream. How could she possibly have been murdered?

High on nervous adrenaline, I hurried up to my room and found Sabine sitting on her bed, working on her needlepoint. Big Saturday night for my roommate. But then, maybe she had the right idea. Going out hadn't exactly been enjoyable for me, to say the least.

"Reed! It's so early," she said, tucking her needlepoint ring away. She sat up and scooted forward, all ears. "How was the date?"

"Awful," I replied. "I left early and walked myself home."

"Oh," she said, sounding overly disappointed.

I whipped off Shelby's coat and started for the closet, but immediately changed my mind and tossed the coat on the foot of my bed instead.

"It's no big deal," I told her, running my fingers through my hair. "So the guy's a jerk. Half the guys at this school are."

"Maybe more than half," Sabine said under her breath.

"What?"

I turned on my computer, more determined than ever to do a little research on Ivy Slade. Now that I had implicated her to the police, I had a sudden desire to back up my claim. To find some kind of evidence that she was, in fact, capable of very bad things.

"Nothing, it's just . . . I was over at Coffee Carma earlier and Missy came in. . . ."

Sabine trailed off, looking squeamish. My heart thumped extra hard. "Missy came in and what?"

"She said she saw Josh and Ivy in front of Pemberly . . . kissing," Sabine said with an apologetic look.

The floor went out from under me, but I quickly grasped at the first straw I thought of. "And you believed her?"

Sabine's brow furrowed. "You think she lied?"

"She's Missy. She hates me. And she would just love to spread a rumor like that."

"Oh. Well, it didn't seem like she was lying," Sabine said. Then, on seeing my face, she quickly added, "But if you think she was, then I'm sure she was."

"I'm sure she was," I affirmed.

I hoped she was. *Please, God, let her be lying.* But I couldn't believe it. I refused to believe it. He couldn't have really moved on so fast. Despite what I'd heard from Jason, I'd thought they were just becoming friends. Close friends. Which sucked, but still. It wasn't as bad as the alternative.

"Reed . . . what exactly happened between you and Josh?" Sabine asked. "No one knows and everyone's speculating. . . . It might help if you talked about it."

"I really don't think so," I replied.

No one was ever going to know that I'd cheated on Josh with Dash. For many, many reasons. Well, aside from the random drunk and stoned partiers in the hallway that night who had witnessed our fight—but apparently none of them had been from Easton or they were just too far gone to remember, because so far, there were no rumors flying around campus. Thank God. If the Billings Girls found out, I was sure that they would be able to forgive me for hurting Josh—they were, after all, my friends, and most of them were dedicated to instant gratification and having fun above all else. But no one would ever forgive me for betraying Noelle. And Noelle, of course, would kill me. That was reason enough.

"Did he cheat on you?" Sabine prompted, toying with her silver ring. "Did he and Ivy hook up at the Legacy or something? Because if he did, that's just reprehensible and I'm glad you dumped him. I mean, how anyone could do that to someone they loved—"

"Sabine, I really don't want to talk about it," I said, cutting her off as the ever-present guilt in my gut started to expand.

"Okay. Sorry," she said quickly, "but if you ever do—"

"I won't. But thanks."

I turned toward my computer and went straight to Google, trying to focus on the task at hand. Trying not to think about Sabine's opinions—about how reprehensible she would find *me* if she knew the truth. I thought about taking out my disc full of info on the Billings Girls, but I didn't want to crack that open in front of Sabine, and I wasn't certain it would have anything on Ivy, since she had never actually *been* a Billings Girl. I could always check it later. For now I was going to search the old-fashioned way.

As Sabine settled in with a book, I Googled Ivy Slade. Luckily, it was not a common name. I got only thirty listings. The first, an obituary.

Victoria Slade, 89
Boston Socialite Was Groundbreaking Feminist

I scrolled through the cached article for Ivy's name and found her listed as one of Olivia's survivors—her granddaughter. Olivia had died over the summer, having suffered a stroke more than a year ago.

Sad. But unhelpful. I closed the obit and went back to my list. There were a couple of mentions of Ivy attending this party or that fund-raiser. Then, jackpot.

The headline: MILLIONAIRE TEEN CAUGHT STEALING . . . FROM OWN MATRIARCH.

I clicked the link, which took me to a Boston gossip site called Dish of Beantown. Okay, not the most reliable source, but I had to see what this was all about.

Sources inside the BPD have confirmed that the "minor" whose name was withheld from the *Boston Globe*'s front-page B&E story yesterday was in fact Boston princess Ivy Slade, 16, daughter of financier Colton Slade and former supermodel Esmeralda Lake-Slade. Apparently home for the weekend from her tony Connecticut boarding school, Easton Academy, Miss Slade got tired of inspecting her diamonds and organizing her couture and decided it might be fun to bust into Grandma's house to snatch God knows what. That pair of Jack Kennedy's boxers the elder Ms. Slade is rumored to have tucked in her trousseau,

perhaps? Too bad the prodigal grandkid never noticed
during all those Sunday teas that Grandma had a state-of-
the-art security system installed. Miss Slade was pinched,
and we're all tickled pink to see what happens next. Is this
the new fave pastime of the rich and semifamous? Better
get out the shotguns, people, before all the kids in the
outers start emulating the fabulous Miss S. We could have
an inept-crime trend on our hands!

I covered my mouth to keep from laughing in shocked glee. Ivy was
arrested for breaking into her own grandmother's house? Why? What
was she hoping to steal? Clearly the girl had everything she needed.
But even more baffling was the fact that the police had yet to investigate her in Cheyenne's death. Didn't a girl with a record—one who was
so intimately connected to the victim—merit a first look?

I sat back in my chair and saved the pertinent files to my hard
drive. At least I had proven one thing—there was definitely something
off with that girl. But was she capable of murder? I couldn't wrap my
brain around that—the idea that there was another student at Easton
who was that evil, that insane. An image of Ariana's cold, hard face
flitted through my mind and a dreadful shiver raced down my spine.

No. There was no way it had happened again. Cheyenne had committed suicide. End of story.

Still, I needed a distraction. Now.

"Sabine?"

She looked up from her book. "Yeah?"

"Do you want to play, like, Spit or something?" I asked her.

"*Absolument!*" she answered brightly, tossing her book aside.

I took a deep breath and grabbed my deck of cards. Thank God there were still a few normal things to do around here. Maybe I should just leave the investigating of potential psychos to the cops.

SO MUCH FOR THAT

Sunday morning dawned crisp and cold. So cold that I had to huddle close to Noelle, Constance, Vienna, and London as we hurried across the leaf-strewn campus toward the dining hall. As the wind whipped my hair back from my face, I burrowed my chin into my scarf and wished I had thought to bring my wool hat. All I wanted to do was get inside again as quickly as possible. All my friends wanted to do was talk about my date.

"I can't believe you walked out on Hunter Braden," Vienna said, clutching London's arm in her shearling coat. "No one walks out on Hunter Braden."

"Reed Brennan does," Noelle said, sounding proud.

"I'm sorry. He's just . . . not my type," I told them, my words muffled by my scarf. I wriggled my chin out and ducked it over the woolly fabric.

"He's everyone's type," London replied.

"Until you talk to him," I told her. "Just trust me. It was the most boring night of my life."

London and Vienna looked at each other and rolled their eyes. "Fine. We'll go to the next candidate," London said, whipping the printed F.Y.R. list out of her pocket. The wind almost made off with it, but she managed to keep it clutched in her gloves. "But if Hunter Braden is boring, I don't really know *who's* going to satisfy you," she added under her breath.

"Who's next?" Constance asked, trying to see over London's shoulder as we walked.

"Dominic Infante. Portia's pick," London replied.

"Actually, I think I'm going to ask out Marc Alberro," I told them.

"You are?" Constance's face lit up.

"Who?" London blurted, looking confused.

"Number fifteen," Vienna informed her, pointing. "Reed, come on. He's, like, a scholarship student."

Noelle snorted a laugh at the faux pas. I stopped in my tracks just outside the door to the dining hall and they all stopped as well. I stared down the blank-faced Twin Cities until they remembered who they were talking to—another scholarship student.

"Oh! Right!" Vienna said finally, blushing. "But this is different. I mean, he's a Dreck."

Dreck was the not-so-positive nickname the Billings Girls had for residents of Drake Hall, the upperclassman dorm where the "unsavory" boys lived.

"Plus he's president of the Purity Club," London said with a shudder, sticking her tongue out like she'd just swallowed a bug.

"Easton has a Purity Club?" I asked, shocked.

"Oh, it's, like, really small," Vienna clarified.

Interesting. I couldn't imagine anyone at this particularly horny school wanting to remain pure, let alone advertise the fact. Marc Alberro was looking better and better. A smart, funny, cute boy with no delusions of grandeur who was not out for sex? Count me in.

"I'm asking him out," I said, whipping open the door and striding into the warm, hustle-bustle of the dining hall.

"Yay!" Constance cheered.

The Twin Cities protested under their breath, but I pretended not to hear. I'd done it their way. Now it was time to try it my way.

I unbuttoned my coat as I walked over to the Billings tables, feeling confident in my decision. Feeling, in fact, better than I had in days. But the feeling was short-lived. Halfway across the cafeteria I noticed people whispering. Eyeing me warily. Glancing away quickly when I looked in their direction. An eerie sense of déjà vu settled in around my shoulders. The vibe in the room was way too familiar. It felt exactly like it had after Thomas's body had been found.

I gulped for air. Cheyenne. Had Easton somehow found out about the murder investigation?

"What's up with the morgue vibe?" Noelle asked, flinging her coat over the back of her chair.

The Billings Girls who were already seated with their meals—
Sabine, Tiff, Rose, Kiki, Astrid, and others—all exchanged nervous looks. Like there was something they didn't want to tell us.
Then Amberly Carmichael scurried over with her two sentries in
tow. She grabbed my forearm with one hand and Noelle's with the
other.

"You guys, I just want you to know, I don't believe a word of it," she
said, her eyes wide and earnest.

"A word of what?" I asked, removing her hand from my arm.

At that moment Missy arrived, dropped her tray on the next table,
and turned around, her arms crossed under her sizable chest.

"You guys should know that everyone's talking about how you
conspired to murder Cheyenne," she said bluntly, looking at me and
Noelle.

I grabbed onto the back of the nearest chair to steady myself.

"What?" Noelle blurted, loud enough that most of the conversation in the airy room screeched to a halt.

"Like I said. Not a word," Amberly repeated. Like it was so important to us that she trusted us. Please. My life was flashing before my
eyes over here.

"*No one* believes a word of it, right, girls? It's crazy talk," Tiffany said,
looking around the table. Everyone murmured their agreement.

"I don't understand. How did this whole thing get started?" Noelle
asked, crossing her arms over her chest.

Everyone at the Billings tables looked around at everyone else.

Again, no one wanted to answer. Finally Missy stepped closer to us and lowered her voice.

"There's a rumor going around that the police questioned someone from school last night," she said. "That they're going to reinvestigate Cheyenne's death."

What? How could anyone know that?

"Now everyone's saying that you got Reed to off Cheyenne so that there would be a vacancy in Billings," Missy added.

Noelle scoffed. "Total fiction. Honestly. Who comes up with this crap?"

"Exactly," Portia added as all our friends nodded and murmured their agreement.

"Everyone's just jealous of you guys. That's why they want to tear you down," Vienna said sagely.

"It's always lonely at the top," Shelby agreed.

"Too true," Noelle said. She looked around the room, taking in the silence and the stares. "Well, this is unacceptable."

She stepped out into the center of the aisle and shook her head incredulously.

"So, you all think Reed and I pulled off a murderous coup at Billings, huh? Do you even hear how ridiculous that sounds?" she announced in a loud voice. "Who would kill someone for a spot in a dorm? Even if it is Billings? Are you guys that hard up for scandal that you're going to believe something like that? I thought that only smart people were admitted to Easton."

There was laughter all around. Her announcement had the desired effect. People went back to their food, and I even caught a few of them rolling their eyes like it really *was* ridiculous. Rumor squelched, just like that. Damn, this girl had power. I wondered if everyone would have believed me if I had said the same thing, but now I'd never get the chance to find out.

"See? I *told* you," Amberly said to her cohorts before ushering them away.

"You do have to admit, the timing was a tad suspect," Missy said casually. "Cheyenne dies and you show up the following week. And after everything that happened last year, people around here think you guys are capable of pretty much anything. You can't really blame them for being suspicious."

"You're going to want to stop talking now," Noelle snapped. Missy did, and took her seat at the next table. She tried and failed to hide a smile behind a cough. The girl was loving every minute of this.

"So who was this mysterious person? Who did the police bring in for questioning?" Sabine wondered aloud, her expression concerned as I slowly unbuttoned my coat.

"Please. It probably didn't even happen," I said, forcing a laugh. "Someone probably made the whole thing up from start to finish."

I glanced up at Noelle as I said this, figuring she'd chuckle and agree with me, but instead her eyes were flat as she stared back at me. My heart all but stopped. She knew. She knew it had been me. She knew I was lying. How did she *do* that?

"Yeah. Probably," Noelle said calmly.

I glanced around at the rest of my friends, feeling suddenly nervous and snagged, but I could tell that Noelle was the one person at the Billings tables who saw through me. The only one who understood that I knew more than I was letting on. And sooner or later, she was going to want to know the truth.

CONTROL

How much could one person handle before totally losing it? This was a question, among many others, that started to plague me after the scene in the dining hall. Not only had I just broken up with my boyfriend, but now he was quite possibly smooching some girl who was a liar with a criminal record and who just generally gave me the creeps. I was hiding the fact that the cause of our breakup was me hooking up with my best friend's boyfriend—though I still didn't know if he was her boyfriend at the time. Meanwhile, someone was planting a dead girl's stuff in my room for sport, and said dead girl might or might not have been murdered. Oh, yeah, and soon the ultra-exclusive dorm of which I was president might be closed down—a travesty for which I would be blamed for all eternity.

Yeah. That wasn't too much to deal with. And I also had classes and calls home to my parents and a rivalry between Sabine and Noelle and my friends forcing me to date random boys.

Public school was starting to look not so bad.

Monday morning I decided that the best thing to do would be to focus on the stuff that I could actually control. Stuff like the fundraiser. So after lunch I went directly to the Crom's office. His assistant, Ms. Lewis, was on the phone when I walked in, looking harried. I waited quietly in front of her desk, thinking of our bizarrely intimate encounters last year, back when she used to be Ms. Lewis-Hanneman. Before her husband had found out she was having an affair with Thomas Pearson's brother Blake. I had been the one person she had confessed everything to. The only person she had managed to trust. It was so strange to think of it now.

Finally she hung up the phone and sighed. She pushed her horn-rimmed glasses up on her nose and smoothed her blond hair back toward her bun, then pulled her chair closer to her desk. "What can I do for you, Miss Brennan?"

"I was hoping to see the headmaster," I said.

She glanced at her phone. One red light was blinking. "He's on his line right now. I can leave him a message."

"I have a few minutes. I can wait," I told her.

"Super," she replied sarcastically. The phone rang again and she quickly answered it. As soon as she hung up, she typed a few words into her computer and yanked a file out of a drawer. She seemed irritated and busy, but while I was there, I did have some business with her as well.

"Ms. Lewis?" I said tentatively.

"Yes?"

She didn't look up as she flipped through some papers in the file.

"I was wondering if you could do me a small favor," I said.

"In all my spare time?" she said.

I laughed quickly for her benefit. "If you get a minute, I mean. I need a list of all the Easton alumni under the age of sixty-five along with their addresses and e-mails."

Ms. Lewis stopped what she was doing and looked up at me like I'd just asked her to put an end to world hunger.

"Come on," I wheedled. "For old times' sake?"

Her glossy lips twisted into a semblance of a smile. "Fine." She grabbed a pen and started to make a note on a Post-it, but there was no ink left. "Nothing is easy today," she said, flinging the pen down and yanking open another drawer. A lockbox slammed forward as she did so. It was labeled—in old, chipped paint—DORM KEYS. Suddenly a lump rose from my chest area into my throat.

"You have keys to all the dorms?" I asked, my blood running cold.

Ms. Lewis quickly slammed the drawer. "Yes. I have to have them so I can make copies when you oh-so-responsible students lose them. Like your friend Kiki did last week."

She gestured at a gray machine atop a filing cabinet behind her. A maker of keys.

"And that's where you keep them? In an unlocked drawer in your desk?"

She clucked her tongue and rolled her eyes. "The lockbox is locked," she said impatiently. "Hence the term *lockbox*."

As she quickly made a note to put together the list I'd asked for, my mind started to roam free. Keys to all the dorms. Right here where anyone could get to them. It wouldn't be that hard, if someone was determined. Dash and I had, after all, broken into this very office last year to use Ms. Lewis's computer. Whoever was messing with me could have easily broken in and stolen the Billings key. Could even have made a copy if they figured out how to work that machine.

Anyone could have the key to Billings. Anyone.

"He's off the phone," Ms. Lewis announced, getting up.

I cleared my throat and attempted to, at the same time, clear my brain. I had to focus now. Cromwell. The passes. I could deal with this new discovery later. Ms. Lewis straightened her skirt and strode over to the double door that connected her office to the headmaster's.

"Reed Brennan to see you, Headmaster," she said as she opened the door.

"What can I do for you, Miss Brennan?" Cromwell asked, not even bothering to look up from the newspaper laid out on his sizable desk.

Ms. Lewis left the two of us alone and I took a deep breath to calm my nerves. His office was blazing hot, as always, thanks to a roaring fire in the ancient fireplace on the far side of the room. The windows were all shut tight, and there was little if any air to be had. How could the man possibly work like this? Had he only recently escaped from hell?

"I'm here to request off-campus passes for this weekend for myself and four fellow students," I told him, hoping that maintaining a formal tone would somehow impress him. I tugged at the collar of my sweater in an attempt to get some air to my skin. It didn't work. "We want to go to New York to finalize plans for our fund-raiser."

"Miss Lange has already applied for, and secured, four passes for this trip," he said, languidly turning the page.

I hesitated. Noelle had already been here? When? And why would she apply for only four when we had already discussed the fact that we needed five?

She was trying to keep Sabine out. Of course she was. How could she have gone behind my back and—

"Was there anything else?" Cromwell asked, still reading.

Okay, focus. Sabine and Noelle were not the issue right now.

"Yes, sir, I'd like one more pass," I said firmly.

Headmaster Cromwell took a deep breath. He looked at his glowing computer screen and hit a few buttons. "Miss Lange has secured passes for you, Miss Simmons, Miss Clarke, and herself. Why, might I ask, are the four of you not enough? Are you in need of someone to carry your bags?"

He looked at me for the first time, a wry smile on his tight lips.

"No, sir," I said patiently. "But we'd like to bring Sabine DuLac with us."

"And why should I let Miss DuLac accompany you?" he asked.

"Because she—"

Okay. "She wants to see New York" wasn't going to fly here. There had to be a plausible reason for Sabine to be in on this trip. Cromwell raised his eyebrows at my hesitation and I noticed the huge globe on its pedestal behind his desk. Epiphany.

"Because Sabine will bring in a lot of international donations," I improvised. "Her family has friends and acquaintances all over the globe. She would be a true asset to the planning committee."

I clasped my sweaty hands together behind my back and prayed my lie would do the trick. Money talked. And international money was still money.

"Fine," Cromwell said finally. "Five passes it is. You can come and pick them up on Friday afternoon."

Yes!

"Thank you, sir. You won't regret this," I said.

"I do hope this project of yours is a success," he said with so little sincerity he was practically transparent.

"And we very much appreciate your support," I replied sarcastically.

Then I turned and walked out of his ovenlike office before my tone had a chance to sink in, and he had a chance to change his mind.

MOOD SWING

It was unbelievable, the lengths Noelle would go to in order to get what she wanted. I knew she didn't like Sabine, but did she hate her so much she couldn't deal with her for one lousy weekend? That seemed so petty. And so beneath Noelle. Couldn't she let me have just one little thing? Couldn't she keep herself from trying to control every aspect of life in Billings?

Well, Noelle clearly didn't realize who she was dealing with. I loved the girl, but she had to get used to the fact that she wasn't the only person living in Billings. Things couldn't always be the way *she* wanted them to be. She had been gone all spring and part of the fall. Did she really think that in all that time, nothing would have changed?

There was already someone at Easton working against me with all this Cheyenne crap—which made my knees jellify every time I thought about it. I didn't need my best friend working against me too.

I shoved through the front door of Hell Hall and jogged down the steps, feeling triumphant and clear for the first time as the cold air hit my face. I was going to have a talk with Noelle. She couldn't go behind my back and change things up on me. I was president of Billings. She was just going to have to get used to it.

I was so focused as I strode across the rapidly darkening campus, I barely noticed Marc sitting on one of the benches in the quad until I was right on top of him.

"Reed, hi," he said, looking up from his French book.

"Marc! Hey," I said, pausing.

The wind tossed my hair in front of my face and I tossed it back with smile. I hadn't seen Marc since I had made the decision to bump him up from number fifteen to number three on the F.Y.R. list. Now I felt as if he'd been placed in my path at the perfect moment. Not only was I high on adrenaline, but I was in definite need of a distraction.

"I'm just studying for a French test," he said. Pointing out the obvious again.

"That's good," I replied.

"What're you up to?" he asked, standing. He was a couple of inches shorter than me, but still beyond cute with his dark hair and light eyes. He wore a gray wool coat with toggle buttons over a burgundy sweater and jeans. Unlike the Ketlar boys, he was not too cool to realize it was freezing out and that he could do something about it. "Have you thought more about the interview? Because I'd really love to get your thoughts on—"

"Actually, yeah. Let's do that. Let's set up a time to do the interview," I replied, adjusting the strap of my bag on my shoulder and tucking my hands underneath my arms to ward off the cold. "How's Wednesday afternoon? Soccer's over, so I'm free."

Marc whipped out a BlackBerry to check his schedule, all business-like. His brows knit as he checked it over. "Wednesday should work. Do you want to—"

"I'll meet you at Coffee Carma at four," I told him, feeling very in charge.

"Four it is," he replied.

"Good. It's a date," I said.

Marc blushed and grinned. It was a nice grin. Real. Not at all smug.

"It's a date," he repeated.

"See you then!"

I turned and walked determinedly toward Billings. I'd dealt with Cromwell and the New York trip, I'd made my next F.Y.R. move. So far, so good. I was taking charge of my life. But as the dorm loomed before me, I started to feel a bit short of breath. Almost dizzy. Almost like I didn't want to go inside.

What if there was something new and unexplained in my room? A few days had gone by since the discovery of Cheyenne's clothing, but rather than making me feel safer, the passing time was making me more paranoid. Who was planting that stuff? What would they do next? And when? When would I open another door or drawer and find some other Cheyenne-related artifact that would knock the wind out of me all over again? All my Noelle-inspired adrenaline started to wane and my steps slowed.

I didn't want to go in there. Didn't want to know what was waiting for me. Billings, the only place that had felt like home in the past year and a half, had changed. All because one of my schoolmates had a very sick, cruel sense of humor. Why would someone want to do this to me? Did I really have such an enemy on campus? What had I done to deserve this?

I paused outside the door and leaned back against it. What if it was someone inside Billings? What if it was more than one person? What if everyone knew what was going on and they were all laughing at me behind my back. What if—

No. Stop. This was my dorm. I was not going to be intimidated. I was not going to be afraid to walk through the door. These were my friends. They wouldn't do this to me. And whatever my mystery stalker wanted to throw at me next, I would just deal with it. Like I'd dealt with Cromwell. I'd deal with it like I knew I could. And whoever was doing this to me would be sorry.

Taking a deep breath, I turned around and strode inside.

TENSION

Everyone was gathered in the parlor. For a fleeting moment I considered just going in there and asking if any of them was behind the black marbles and the clothing, and maybe even how that picture of Cheyenne and me had made it out of my desk drawer and onto my bulletin board a few weeks back—which I was starting to think was part of all this. Or if any of them was helping someone on the outside. Just call them out. But then I realized that revealing what was going on to the general Billings population would be a mistake. It would make me look weak. It would bring up questions about why I was the only one being targeted. I would have to tell them about the e-mail. About my guilt. And I was not about to do that.

No, I was just going to have to figure this out on my own. Once the fund-raiser was over. Once everything started to normalize again. Then I would deal with my tormentor.

Decision made, I walked over to the parlor door and instantly my blood started to boil. Noelle was standing in front of the fireplace, addressing a rapt audience of Billings Girls. Clearly, this was a formal meeting and clearly, Noelle was in charge.

"So if your parents want to fly in anyone from the West Coast, let me know by Friday. Daddy's going to let us use his jet for one cross-continental run, so we'll need to make sure everyone knows where to be and when," Noelle was saying. A few people made a note of this and Noelle glanced at the next item on her agenda. She had an agenda. "Okay, now—"

"What's going on?" I said loudly, announcing my presence to the room.

Everyone turned around. My irritation must have been evident, because many of them looked quickly, guiltily away.

"Reed! Good. There you are. We were just going over some of the details for the fund-raiser," Noelle said, unfazed. "I went to Cromwell about the off-campus passes and he said four is the limit, so we're back to the original plan." She turned to Sabine and shrugged. "Sorry, Frenchie. You're out."

Sabine's face fell, which made me want to scream. Or hit something. Possibly Noelle.

"Actually, *I* just talked to Cromwell and secured the extra pass," I said pointedly, my skin burning with barely suppressed ire. "So Sabine, you're still in."

Everyone looked from me to Noelle, as if we were volleying in a tennis match. Noelle's lips screwed up in something that vaguely resembled a smile. "Well. I guess your powers of persuasion are improving."

All the faces swiveled to me.

"Yeah. I guess they are," I replied.

Silence. I had silenced Noelle. Cool. I walked into the room, dropping my bag and coat on the window seat, and joined Noelle up front. "So, has anyone had any new ideas about the theme?" I asked.

Everyone looked at everyone else. There was so much tension in the room, I was surprised any of us could breathe.

"Reed, can I talk to you for a second?" Noelle said through her teeth, but maintaining a sunny tone. "Alone?"

"Sure," I replied, just as sunnily. "Why don't you guys brainstorm while we're gone? Constance, would you take notes?"

As Noelle followed me out of the room, I knew there would be no talk of the fund-raiser. All they were going to talk about was me and Noelle, and take bets on who might throw the first bitch slap.

THE TRUTH

I led Noelle right into my room and whirled on her the moment she closed the door behind us. I was so full of pent-up emotion that I was able to shove my fear of being there all the way to the back of my mind.

"What the hell was that? You're calling meetings behind my back now?" I demanded. God, it felt good to yell. It felt like all the confusion and stress were pouring right out of me.

"This is not about the fund-raiser. Screw the fund-raiser," Noelle replied, stepping toward me. "This is about Cheyenne."

Instantly, my ballooned-up ego deflated to nothing. Determination, gone. Anger, gone. I glanced at my closed closet door.

"What about Cheyenne?" I asked quietly.

"I'm only going to ask you this once, Reed," Noelle said, crossing her arms over her chest. "Did you have anything to do with Cheyenne's death?"

My heart dropped through my body so quickly I felt faint. "What?" I breathed.

"I need to know the truth. I'm not going to go through what I went through last year," Noelle said coolly. "Not again."

I turned away from her accusing eyes, my mind reeling. I couldn't focus on anything, and the details of my room seemed to circle in front of me. The window, the desk, the photo of me and Scott, my bedspread, my lamp, the window, the desk—everything swirled.

"You can't really think . . . you can't really think that I could do something like that."

"That's not an answer, Reed. I know you were the one the police brought in for questioning. Don't even try to deny it," she said. "So what the hell was that all about?"

"It was nothing," I lied. My back was to her and I started to empty my bag just to give myself something to do. Give me an excuse not to look her in the eye. "It was just . . . they never interviewed me after Cheyenne was found. I left campus with Josh and they questioned everyone else in the dorm, but they never questioned me. They just wanted to make sure they had everyone's accounts of what happened. You know, for the file."

"And that was it," Noelle said, sounding unconvinced. "They didn't say anything about Cheyenne being murdered. Didn't ask if you had anything to do with it."

Her doubtful tone caused something to snap inside of me, and I turned around. "How could you think—"

"Allow me to quote from an e-mail you sent to a certain someone we both know," she replied, as still as stone. "'Cheyenne has lost it. We need to find a way to get rid of her. I need your help.' Now what was that all about?"

Holy. Holy. Crap. Had Noelle just quoted to me from one of my e-mails to Dash? That was it. I could no longer stand. I fell back onto the edge of my bed and put my head between my knees, fighting for breath. The past few months flashed before my eyes. E-mails with Dash. Phone calls. His desperation that night at the Driscoll dinner. The longing in his brown eyes as he pulled me to him at the Legacy. Was it all lies? One big game? Had he told Noelle everything? Had he been betraying me at every turn?

"How did you . . . ?" I lifted my head. Noelle's expression was a mask of disgust. I closed my eyes for a moment, letting an extreme head rush pass. "You know about . . . you know I e-mailed Dash?"

Suddenly I no longer cared about Noelle's power-tripping. All I cared about was making it up to her. Explaining it to her. Keeping her from hating me.

Noelle scoffed, looking up at the ceiling like she just couldn't figure out what to do with me. "Reed, try to remember who you're talking to. I read every last one of your pathetic e-mails and every one of his," Noelle replied. "Dash and I have no secrets. Even when we're broken up, I know his every move. This isn't just some high school crush. Dash and I are meant to be together. One little breakup is not going to derail that. And you"—she paused to laugh derisively—"you, Glass-Licker, are certainly not going to derail that."

"So . . . what? He showed them to you?" I said, finding some indignation toward Dash in the midst of all my mind-bending panic. Did she know about the Legacy? Did she know?

"Please. No. I've known his password since freshman year. He never changes it," she replied. "So while we were apart, I kept an eye on him. Had to make sure my man was staying out of trouble."

Wow. I knew the girl liked to have her control, but wasn't spying on her ex-boyfriend's e-mails going a little far over the line into complete paranoia? Although, in this case she'd had every reason to be paranoid.

"So, yes. I know all about your little flirtation," she told me with a superior glint in her eye. "You should know by now, Reed, that you can't keep secrets from me."

"Noelle, it didn't mean anything," I told her quickly, standing. "It was just stupid and—"

Noelle laughed merrily. "Please. I'm not worried about you and Dash flirting on your computers like some pathetic fourth-graders. Could you be any lamer?"

My face burned as if I'd just been slapped.

"He just missed me and you were a distraction. I know neither of you would ever have the balls to actually *do* anything," she added. "Neither one of you is that stupid."

Implication? If we had "done something," she would have made us pay. So she didn't know every move he made. She didn't know what had happened at the Legacy. As relief flooded through me, so did an intense desire to tell her everything we had done—to wipe that superior certainty off her condescending face and show her that she

did not know everything. But I bit my tongue. Even in all the trauma
of the moment, my self-preservation instinct kicked in.

Leave well enough alone.

"Let's get back to the point," Noelle directed, walking over to my
desk. She picked up my plastic box of paper clips and toyed with it,
dumping the contents back and forth slowly, like a rattle. "You wanted
to get rid of Cheyenne, so tell me . . . what did you do?"

"I wanted to get her expelled, not killed," I replied, turning my palms
out at my sides. "She was out of control . . . treating the new girls like
dirt . . . trying to get *them* thrown out of school. I was actually e-mailing
Dash to see if he could get in touch with *you* for help. Since you—"

I paused, not wanting to dredge up any more unpleasant memories. Noelle's brown eyes lit with understanding.

"Since I got Leanne expelled last year," Noelle finished, placing
the box down again. "That was really more Ariana's thing."

"I know, but Noelle . . ." I gazed at her, on the verge of desperate
tears. "Honestly, did you really think I could ever kill someone? I mean,
you know me."

She glanced at me out of the corner of her eye. "I knew Ariana
too," she said. "Or so I thought. I'm not making that blind-trust mistake again."

Okay. She had a point. But it wasn't fair that Ariana's insanity
should prejudice Noelle against me. I hadn't done anything wrong.
Well, not anything that could get me arrested, anyway.

"Cheyenne and I were not getting along toward the end. Everyone knows this," I told her. "But I had nothing to do with her death.

I mean, just look at it logically. The girl was out. She was expelled. I was never going to have to see her again. Why would I kill her?"

Noelle turned to face me fully and studied my face for a long moment. I couldn't believe she was still doubting me. Me. Her best friend.

"Noelle, please. You have to believe me," I said, my voice cracking. "I can't lose you, too."

Finally, Noelle rolled her eyes and gave me a genuine smile. "Aw, Glass-Licker, you're such a sap," she said, tilting her head to the side.

"Could you *please* stop calling me Glass-Licker?" I asked, grasping at levity.

"No," she replied. "You flirted with my boyfriend. I get to call you whatever I want for as long as I want."

Right. I guess I couldn't argue with that.

"But we're okay?" I asked uncertainly.

"We're okay," she replied. "Let's go back downstairs before those girls decide on a slumber party theme without our direction."

"Good idea."

She walked ahead of me out of my room and I paused for a moment to collect myself. My heart was racing, my mind felt numb, and there was a cool sheen of sweat all over my skin. The only question in my mind right then was how long we would be okay. How long could a person like Noelle Lange be kept in the dark about what really happened at the Legacy? And how long would I survive if she ever found out?

THANK NOELLE

I had to focus on the task at hand. Focus. Not on Josh, not on Noelle, not on the Cheyenne investigation. On the fund-raiser. Focus on the fund-raiser. It was about all I could do to keep myself sane.

So after English lit class on Tuesday, Sabine and I speed-walked to lunch to go over our short list of theme ideas, which we had narrowed down at the meeting the night before. By the end of the day I was going to make a decision. By the end of the day something was going to be set in stone.

We grabbed sandwiches and bottled water and got to our table before any of the other Billings Girls arrived. In fact, the place was as still as the library. Only a few of the faculty and some of the foreign exchange students—who always seemed to arrive early to everything— were present, and their conversations were whispered, hushed.

"I think 'indulgence' is a perfect theme," Sabine whispered as we sat down. "All those ideas London had about serving only sweets and champagne and having private massage rooms and cashmere blankets on every seat as favors—it sounded divine."

"I like it too, but it might be too expensive to pull off. It'll all depend on whether or not the Twin Cities can really get all that stuff for free or at cost," I replied, opening my notebook to the theme list. "What about the green theme? The environment is so trendy right now and we—"

"Ladies! I've got it!"

I stopped talking as the door to the dining hall flew open and Noelle made her announcement. She strode over to our table, her cheeks flushed from the cold, tugging her camel-colored suede gloves from her fingers. Tiffany, London, Vienna, Portia, and Shelby were at her heels, looking like very excited ladies-in-waiting.

"You've got what?" I asked, looking up at Noelle as she paused at the end of the table.

"The most perfect fund-raiser idea ever!" She shrugged her thick hair off her shoulders and spread her fingers wide. "We are going to make so much money for this school, the Crom will not only leave Billings alone, he'll bow down to us for the rest of our scholastic lives."

I glanced warily at Sabine, whose expression had turned hard and cold. No surprise there. I was sure she saw this as yet another attempt by Noelle to seize control of Billings. But even if I did feel a twinge of foreboding myself, I had to ignore it. I owed Noelle that much, after last night's conversation. Besides, I was kind of psyched to hear about this plan of hers. In my experience Noelle's plans were generally fabulous.

"Don't keep us in suspense," I prompted.

"Right. So we have the big, extravagant dinner for the per-plate donation we talked about, but we also offer a special platinum ticket," Noelle said, pulling a chair over to sit at the head of the table.

"And what do they get with a platinum ticket?" I asked.

"Patience, Reed. I was getting to that," Noelle said with a condescending smile. "Anyone buying a platinum ticket will be invited to a salon earlier in the day to be styled by the one and only Frederica Falk, stylist to the stars."

London and Vienna clasped hands and squealed at the sound of the name. Like Noelle had just announced that Brad Pitt was going to be teaching their afternoon art history class.

"*And* photographed by Tassos, world-renowned fashion photographer," Tiffany added, grinning.

"Really? That's amazing," I said.

I had never heard of Frederica Falk, but all the other girls seemed beside themselves at the mention of her name. And I knew from the reverent way the Billings Girls talked about Tiffany's father, Tassos, that landing a shoot with him was one of the most sought-after prizes of the rich and famous. We could make a killing with this.

"And Dad has offered to donate a whole slew of his old photos and cameras and equipment so that we can auction them off at the dinner," Tiffany added, dropping into the chair next to mine. She whipped her heather gray scarf off and opened her coat. "He can't wait. Said the studios are long overdue for a purging."

"Are you sure he's okay with this?" I asked, turning to her. "I know he's usually pretty busy."

"Yeah, but he knows how much Billings means to me, so he's going to clear his weekend," Tiffany said with a shrug of her slim shoulders. "He even said he'll donate all the film and developing, so his involvement won't cost us a thing."

"Wow. This is amazing," I said, dollar signs floating through my head.

"Frederica's donating her time too," Noelle added as the other girls took off their coats and slung them over various chairs with their bags. "Kiran had major dirt on the woman, so it wasn't exactly difficult to convince her to go along."

"Wait a minute. Kiran's involved? You talked to her?" I asked, nearly breathless at the thought. Kiran Hayes had been one of my best friends last year before the whole Thomas scandal went down, and I hadn't heard from her since. Suddenly I was practically salivating for news. "How is she?"

"She's fine. She's Kiran," Noelle said with a blasé wave of her hand. "Living with some male model on the Left Bank . . . planning some psychotic birthday bash for herself in Amsterdam or something. The usual."

My friends chuckled knowingly, but I couldn't believe that was all I was getting. The girl had dropped off the face of the earth, except for the occasional appearance in a perfume ad or magazine spread. Had she finished school? Did she care? Was she still drinking like a fiend, or had she gotten her crap together? Info, please! "Anyway, Frederica is going to bring along five assistants to make sure everything runs smoothly, and since she owns her own makeup line, supplies won't be a problem," Noelle said, shrugging out of her cashmere coat. "This is going to be *the* event of the season."

"Try the year," Portia corrected.

"I don't know what to say, you guys," I told them, feeling awed by their abilities, their connections. "This is going to be incredible."

"Well, thank Noelle," Shelby said, tucking her iPhone away and shaking her blond hair back. "It was all her idea."

I glanced at Sabine again. She could have incinerated the entire dining hall with the fire in her eyes.

"Come on. I'm starved," Portia said, grabbing a potato chip off my plate. "Let's motor."

As Noelle, Tiffany, Portia, Shelby, and the Twin Cities scurried off to secure their lunches, I found myself alone with Sabine—and I didn't relish it. I had a feeling I was in for another overly concerned lecture.

"Please don't tell me you think Noelle is trying to oust me again," I said, taking a bite of my sandwich. "Anyone could have come up with that idea."

"Yes, but 'anyone' didn't," Sabine said, throwing in some air quotes. I had never seen her use air quotes before. She was really becoming Americanized. "Noelle did. And she should have at least run it past you before telling everyone how brilliant she is."

"She had to tell Tiffany, at least, so that Tiff could ask her father right away," I replied. "And besides, who cares who knew first? We were all going to hear it eventually."

"It's a matter of respect," Sabine said firmly. "She has no respect for you."

My mouth went dry and I took a long drink from my water bottle. Unfortunately, Sabine's blunt comment struck a nerve. Noelle had always been my friend, but she had rarely, if ever, shown any respect for me—well, except for that night when she'd saved my life.

"Aw. Madame President is looking a tad peaked," Ivy Slade said, stopping next to our table with her tray. "Having trouble finding people who want to help you save the Den of Evil?"

I wanted to reply, but not a single comeback came to mind. Ivy grinned at my hesitation, then laughed in my face and sauntered off toward Josh's table. I watched her go with narrowed eyes, wishing I had some kind of telekinetic power that could send her sprawling on her ass from across the room. Clearly, Hauer hadn't brought her in for questioning yet, or she couldn't possibly be so smug.

Or maybe she could. Who knew? The girl was a complete enigma. Noelle had been no help, and I assumed that the rest of the Billings Girls would be mum about Ivy as well. If one member of my house thought something was big enough to keep a secret, that usually meant they all agreed. But someone else at this school had to know something more about her. Someone who would be willing to talk.

TOTALLY WRONG

"I've been doing a lot of research on the subject, and the residents of Billings House have always sort of pushed the envelope around here with the administration turning a blind eye. Why do you think they're coming down so hard on you now?"

I stared at Marc's digital recorder, which he held in front of my face. Suddenly I realized I should have given some thought to what he might ask me and what I might say in return. But how was I supposed to concentrate on such things with so much going on around me?

"Reed?" Marc prompted.

"Um . . . because the new headmaster is a repressed jackass who's probably never experienced a single moment of unadulterated fun in his entire sad life?" I blurted.

Marc looked at me, startled, then cracked up laughing. He doubled over and I felt a laugh bubble up in my throat as well. Before long we were both laughing uncontrollably in the middle of the sunlit quad.

"Can I quote you on that?" he asked, his eyes glistening with merry tears.

"Probably not a good idea," I replied, grabbing his recorder and turning it off.

It took a minute for us to regain our breath. It felt so good to laugh, I wanted to keep doing it all afternoon, but then I saw something that brought me up short, and my mirth died. Just like that. It was Detective Hauer, and he was striding purposefully across the quad a number of yards off. I glanced ahead, checking where he was going, and my eyes fell on Josh. Josh, who was walking toward Ketlar, completely oblivious to the heat-seeking missile coming his way. All the blood rushed out of my head.

"Reed? Are you all right?" Marc asked, concerned.

I didn't answer. Couldn't. What did Hauer want with Josh? The detective caught Josh's attention, and Josh looked around for a moment, as if disbelieving that the man was talking to him. He looked so skittish, so frightened in that moment, I just wanted to go over there and get between them. Protect Josh from whatever was about to happen.

Marc turned around and saw what had caught me so off guard. We both watched as Hauer led Josh back to Hell Hall. Watched until they disappeared inside.

"What's going on? Why would the police want to talk to Josh?" I said, breathless.

"It makes sense. He and Cheyenne were involved in that whole drug-sex scandal thing right before she died," Marc said pragmatically.

"Maybe they think he was holding it against her or something."

"You know about that?" I demanded.

Marc hesitated for a moment, as if snagged. Had he been research-
ing me and my past as well as Billings? "Doesn't everyone know about
that?" he said finally.

I supposed it was possible. News did travel fast at Easton. Especially scandalous news. I decided to let it go. Especially considering
there were more urgent matters at hand.

"So you think he's a *suspect*?" I asked, my heart racing.

"*I* don't," Marc clarified. "But *they* might."

"This is insane. I can't believe they're doing this to him again,"
I said, my words coming out in a rush. "The girl committed suicide.
Josh didn't do anything. He wouldn't. He—"

"Reed, it's okay. You don't know what they're doing in there. I'm
sorry I said anything," Marc told me, turning around and straddling
the bench so he could face me fully. "Don't jump to conclusions,
okay? I'm sure it's fine."

I had told Hauer to question Ivy. Ivy, not Josh. Had he just completely ignored everything I said?

"Reed, if you want to do this interview some other time, I completely understand," Marc was saying.

Off to my left, I heard a familiar laugh. Gage's laugh. I glanced over
at him, hanging with some of his Ketlar boys. Gage, of course. Gage
had dated Ivy last year, had been fooling around with her as recently
as two weeks ago. If there was anyone on this campus who knew about
Ivy, it was him.

"I'm really sorry, Marc. I have to go," I said, standing and gathering up my book bag and coffee cup. "Rain check?"

"Sure," he said, standing as well. "Do you want me to walk you back to your—"

But I didn't let him finish. I was already halfway to Gage. When I reached him, I grabbed the arm of his trendy wool sweater and dragged him away from his friends.

"Backwater Brennan! What's with the stealth attack?" he asked, yanking his arm away. At first he looked annoyed, but then his eyes lit with conceited understanding. "Oh, am I your next conquest?" he asked, rubbing his hands together as he looked me up and down. "Sweet."

"Ew. No."

I swallowed back the bile that was oozing its way up my throat and yanked him down next to me on an empty bench. Gage was, of course, unfazed by my response.

"I have a question about Ivy," I told him.

"You mean Ice-Cold Bitch?" he said, clenching his jaw as he looked away. Apparently, someone was holding a grudge against his former paramour. Interesting. I hadn't been aware that Gage was capable of feelings. Maybe he'd recently seen the Wizard about a heart. "What about her?"

"What happened to her last year?" I asked. "Why didn't she come back to Easton for her junior year?"

"You know, jealousy doesn't become you, Reed," Gage told me, his blue eyes sparkling. "You want to get back at Hollis, don't go sniffing around about his new lady friend. You have to make *him* jealous. And I can help with that," he said suggestively, eyeing my legs.

God. What was with the guys around here?

"Did you not catch the 'ew, no'?" I asked him, snapping my knees together. "Now spill."

Gage rolled his eyes and sighed. "Fine. Whatever. I'd only be the best you ever had, but your loss. Ivy's grandmother got sick toward the end of our sophomore year, and she and Ivy were, like, really close, so Ivy decided to go to some school in Boston to be close to her. Then this summer the old lady croaked and voilà. The prodigal bitch returns to Easton to wreak havoc on all our lives." He opened his palms toward the sky with a wry smile. "Happy now?" he asked.

Not exactly. This did not add up at all. Ivy as caring granddaughter? Ivy giving up her whole school life to be there for a member of her family? That so didn't track with the girl I knew. The girl who was always ready with an obnoxious comment. The girl who had tried to keep all of Easton out of the most exclusive party of the year. The girl who had allegedly broken into said grandmother's house intending to steal something. The girl who had dropped a guy who clearly liked her and gone after *my* guy before I'd had even a day to mourn our relationship.

"One more question," I said, unable to stop myself.

"Make it quick. I have to take a piss before my club meeting," Gage said.

Charming.

"Are Ivy and Josh . . . are they, like, serious?" I asked, filleting my heart down the middle and leaving it wide open to his answer.

Gage looked at me for a moment, and for that one moment I swear I saw actual compassion in his eyes.

"Please. Ivy is never serious about anyone," he said, standing. Then he turned and faced me and opened his arms. "Besides, the girl does have a brain. She'll be coming back for more of *this* in no time."

Gag. But still. I hoped he was right.

"Has everyone come up with a guest list?" I asked that night. Via e-mail, I had reminded each of my Billings sisters that they were to create their own lists of invitees for the fund-raiser—friends, family, people with cash. We were getting down to the wire, so I hoped that everyone had made time to work on it between classes.

"Got it!" Portia announced, holding up her rhinestone-covered PDA as everyone else murmured their assent.

"Mine's handwritten. Is that bad?" Constance asked, biting her lip.

"It doesn't matter what format it's in as long as you have one," I replied. "Now I need someone to volunteer to compile them all and cross-reference for any duplicates. Volunteers?"

"I'll do it!" Kiki offered. Her mouth was full of the mini éclair she'd just popped into it, but I got the gist. Vienna had ordered up a few dozen delicacies from the French bakery in town, which were now being passed around on silver platters.

"Great. Everyone get your lists to Kiki by the end of the night," I directed. "We'll also be inviting every Easton alumni under the age of sixty-five. Ms. Lewis e-mailed me the list today, and I'll forward that to you as well," I told Kiki.

"Okay," Kiki said, taking Constance's list. "What do I do with all the addresses once I have them?"

"Actually, I was kind of hoping that maybe you and Astrid could come up with some kind of gorgeous e-mail invite to send to everyone," I replied. "We can mock it up now and then just add in the locations once we have them. Sound good?"

"I'm in!" Astrid announced.

"I just got this new design software from my dad that's still in prototype. It's killer," Kiki added.

Noelle sat forward in her chair and cleared her throat. "E-mail? Really?" she asked, looking up at me like I had suggested finger-painting the invites. "Isn't that sort of gauche?"

I felt my fingers start to curl. I had decided to go with her theme. Did she really have to contradict my one piece of input in front of everyone? I mean, I know I had flirted with her man and all, but did that mean I was never going to get a say in anything ever again?

No. I wouldn't let her step all over me that way. So I'd flirted with Dash. Last year she'd helped kidnap my boyfriend and had left him for dead. I'd say we were even. Until she found out about the fact that

I'd almost slept with Dash. That might tip the scales in her view. But as of now, she didn't know about that.

"It's the fastest and cheapest way to reach everyone," I told her patiently. "If we have to get invitations printed and stamped and mailed, by the time the guests receive them, it will be two days before the party."

Noelle raised her palms. "Point taken."

I let out a breath. See? She wasn't trying to control things. She was simply voicing an opinion. Way to overreact, Reed.

"Okay, I think that's it for tonight," I told the room. "If anyone has any suggestions for us before we leave for New York on Saturday, stop by my room and let me know."

The meeting broke up with everyone gabbing happily and comparing their lists, swiping a few more treats from the platters around the room. I suddenly felt too exhausted to move. It was difficult, keeping up appearances and being a leader when my mind was on Josh and Hauer and a million other things. It took a lot out of me. Noelle stood, selected a small tart, and wrapped it in a linen napkin to bring with her upstairs. I had been hoping for a moment alone with her and was glad she had hung back from the crowd.

"I swear, with the amount of crap we've been consuming at these meetings, the eating disorders in this place are about to skyrocket," she joked.

"Noelle," I said, wiping my palms on my wool skirt, "have you heard anything about Detective Hauer meeting with Josh this afternoon?"

Noelle smiled sympathetically. "Worried about the boy who dumped you? You're so sweet."

The boy who dumped me? I'd never told anyone that was how it had happened. Did she know, or did she just assume? Did she know more about that night than she had let on?

"I didn't—"

"I'm just messing with you," Noelle said, stepping toward me. "I heard it was just a routine questioning. Because apparently she used the same stuff to off herself as she used to mess with him. There's an obvious connection."

Obvious. Obvious that Cheyenne was a nut job who was capable of anything. Why wouldn't they just chalk her death up to suicide and let it go?

"Besides, didn't you say you both left campus before they had a chance to question you?" Noelle asked, arching her brows. "Maybe they're just now catching up with Hollis as well. If, of course, that was really the reason for your visit with the police the other night."

My face turned warm. I felt as if she could see right into my brain. "Right. That makes sense."

Noelle smirked, then instantly shifted gears. "Don't worry, Reed. He'll be fine," she said kindly, soothingly. "He can take care of himself."

"I know." Or maybe Ivy was taking care of him.

"Come on. You can help me with my Spanish. You're one of those dorks who love homework, right?" she joked, knocking me with her arm as she passed me by.

"I'll be right up," I told her.

I hoped she was right—I hoped Josh was fine without me—but the idea that he could be only made my heart ache worse. As much as I was trying to move on and cling to my anger with him over Ivy, I hated not knowing what was going on with him. I hated not being able to be there for him. I hated myself for doing this to us.

LIFE AFTER HOLLIS

I had never been inside a Drake Hall common room before. It was nice. Cozy. There was a fire in the old stone fireplace, big leather chairs all around the room, and the walls were paneled in dark wood. It had the feel of a mountain lodge. Not that I'd ever been to a mountain lodge, but I imagined this was how it would feel. Unlike the common room on Josh's floor in Ketlar, there was no big-screen TV or boys shouting over a round of Guitar Hero in the corner. The few guys dotted around the room were studying, carrying on whispered debates.

This was where the real students lived.

"So, where are you from, anyway?" I asked Marc. I leaned over the open Tupperware box on the table between us, chose one of the flaky, homemade desserts his mother had sent him, and leaned back in my comfy leather chair.

"We're supposed to be interviewing you," Marc reminded me.

"I'm bored of me," I replied. "Let's talk about you for a while."

Marc smiled and turned off the recorder, which sat next to the Tupperware. "I have one more question first, off the record," he said.

"Sure," I replied, licking some powdered sugar from my lower lip. Whatever I was eating was damn good.

"Is this an interview or a date?" he asked.

My heart skipped a surprised beat. "What makes you think it's a date?"

Marc looked at the floor and rubbed his hands together shyly. He glanced up with a tentative expression. "Constance said something about a list. . . ."

I laughed and finished off my little pastry. "Trust Constance to stick her nose in. So maybe it is a date." I didn't want it to be a date. Not really. I didn't want to be on a date with anyone other than Josh. But that was what this was supposed to be. So I said it. "Is that okay with you?"

His eyebrows shot up. "Very okay."

I felt a bit guilty after that. Like I was giving him false hope. But I soldiered on.

"Good. So where are you from?" I asked again, reaching for another pastry.

"Miami," he replied.

I paused mid-bite. When I thought of Miami, I thought of neon lights, hot pink spandex, and loud music. Marc was none of these things. His very being screamed New Englander. "Really? But you're so—"

"Preppy? Ambitious? Sober?" he supplied.

"Okay," I said.

"I never really fit in there," he told me. He leaned back in his chair and laid his arms on top of the chair arms, then started to tap a beat on the front of them with both hands. "My older brother, Carlos, was born to live there. All my friends worshipped him because he, you know, raced cars and knew all the bouncers and had a different girl over every night and never seemed to actually work a day. They thought he was the coolest thing ever. I just thought it was sad. I couldn't wait to get out of there."

"Wow," I said.

"Too much information?" he asked.

"No. Not at all. It just sounds familiar," I replied.

"You have a slutty, drag-racing older brother?" Marc joked.

I laughed and reached for my coffee cup. "No. Not that part. Just the part where you couldn't wait to get out of there."

"Didn't fit in out there in central Pennsylvania?" he asked.

My paranoia flared instantly. "How did you know where I was from?"

"Reed, I'm a reporter. I'm doing a story on you. Come on," he said, turning his palms up.

"I thought the story was more about Billings."

"Yeah, and you're president of Billings. The girl who's single-handedly trying to save it," Marc said. Like, *duh*. "You're kind of central to the story."

"Oh. Right." I laughed.

And as I laughed I realized that I only ever laughed anymore when

I was with Marc. I looked at him and he looked at me and I felt nothing. Zero tingle. Zero attraction. Zero emotion. He wasn't Josh, but I liked being with him. It made me forget the other stuff. There was a definite possibility that this guy could be a good friend.

"So. How big's *your* scholarship?" he asked with a wry smile.

"Like I'd ever tell you that," I responded, and smacked his arm lightly.

"I'll get it out of you eventually," he told me, reaching for one of the pastries. "It's what I do."

I sipped my coffee and settled in. We spent the next hour talking about how surreal it was to be at Easton without trust funds behind us. Our hopes of breaking into the Ivy League. The crazy birthday gifts our parents cobbled together during leaner years. In the end it was one of the most enjoyable nights I'd had in recent memory. And he didn't even try to kiss me at the door.

As I strolled away from Drake Hall, I felt somehow lighter. I knew that there was definitely going to be life after Josh Hollis. Maybe not with Marc, but with someone. Someday. Maybe even soon. It was actually possible.

CRAZY

Friday night was movie night at Billings—at least, for those who didn't have dates or visiting parents. As I approached my dorm, I saw the dim glow of the plasma screen through the front window of the parlor and knew that most of my friends were inside, riveted to whatever words of wisdom Cameron Diaz or Reese Witherspoon were imparting this week. I yanked open the outer door of the dorm and paused. The inner door was ajar, propped open with the bronze doorstopper that was only ever used on move-in day to facilitate the passage of huge suitcases and trunks. The red security light on the keycard slot was blinking and emitting a low, ineffective beep, annoyed that the door had been ajar for too long. What was it doing open? And why hadn't anyone noticed?

I stepped inside and nudged the heavy doorstopper aside with my foot, then quietly closed the door. I could see Sabine, Constance, and Kiki sitting in the parlor with their hair spilling over the back of one of the couches. Nothing seemed amiss. Part of me wanted to go in there and ask them about the door, but if I did, I knew that Constance would pump me for the details of my date, so instead I quickly slipped upstairs.

Big mistake. The second I opened the door to my room, I froze. Literally. It was freezing inside. Something moved in the dark. Fear instantly overcame me and I slammed the door, pressing myself up against the wall outside. Someone was in there. Someone was in my room.

My heart was in my throat. Why would someone be skulking around in my room in the dark? Were they leaving another surprise for me? Or did they have something even worse planned? Whoever was in there knew I was out here now. We were playing a waiting game. Him or her in there. Me out here. Who would crack first?

Ever so slowly, I turned and pressed my ear to the door to see if I could hear the culprit moving around inside. I held my breath. There was nothing. Dead silence. Was this person on the other side of the door right now . . . listening for me?

Why were they doing this to me? What had I done to deserve this?

Down the hall, a door opened and laughing voices emerged. I looked up to find Lorna and Missy walking out of the Twin Cities' room with a bunch of folded blankets. They stopped in their tracks at the sight of me still bundled in my coat, my gloved hands pressed into the door along with my left ear.

"What are you doing?" Missy asked with a sneer.

Freaking out. Losing my mind. Having a panic attack.

"Someone's in my room," I whispered.

"Sabine?" Lorna asked at full voice.

I felt so desperate I wanted to cry. But at least I had backup now. At least if I opened the door, they would see there was someone in there too. I'd have witnesses.

"No. Sabine's downstairs," I whispered hoarsely. "I think some-one's sneaking around my room."

"Like who?" Missy asked. "Everyone's in the parlor."

I pressed my lips together. I hated that of all the people in Billings, it was Missy who had to be here for this, but she was better than no one. "I don't know. Maybe someone from outside Billings," I said, thinking of the open door. "Will you guys please just go in there with me?"

Lorna looked a little freaked, but she nodded resolutely. "Sure."

"Thanks." I turned slowly, trying not to make any noise, and silently turned the knob. "One, two, three," I whispered. Then I flung the door open. Wide open. And braced myself for some kind of attack. I didn't even realize I had closed my eyes until Missy shoved me aside from behind and I was startled into looking around.

"There's no one in here," she said, flicking on the light.

She was right. The room was deserted.

"No, but it's freezing," Lorna added. She dropped the blankets onto my bed and walked across to my window, which was wide open. The wind coming through the ever-present screen sent the curtains billowing into the room.

The curtains. That must have been what I had seen. The curtains moving.

As Lorna slammed and locked the window, my face burned with embarrassment. I was turning into a paranoid freak. And Missy Thurber and Lorna Gross had been there to witness it.

"There's no one in the bathroom, either," Lorna said, checking it.

I turned and checked both closets, now almost hoping I'd find some psycho lurking about. Anything to make me look like less of a paranoid delusional nutcase. But there was nothing.

"You don't get enough attention around here?" Missy said with a smirk. "Now you have to create fake stalkers? Poor, poor President Reed. Always such a victim."

"You know, you're even uglier on the inside than you are on the outside," I snapped.

Missy's jaw dropped. For a split second I actually thought she was going to cry, and I didn't even care. I was too pent up, frustrated, and embarrassed to care. And besides, why did she always have to be so rude? She had no idea what was going on in my life. No clue. And did she care? No. She just lived to attack me.

"You are such a bitch," she said through her teeth. "You may have everyone else around here snowed, but I know the nice-girl thing is all an act, and sooner or later you're going to get yours, Reed. Just wait."

She stomped out of my room with her blankets, leaving Lorna

hovering behind. Was that a threat? Had Missy just threatened me? And why had she used the word *stalker*? I hadn't said anything about a stalker. Just that I thought someone was in my room. Did she know I had a stalker because she *was* the stalker?

Fab. Now my brain was starting to hurt.

"Are you okay?" Lorna asked me quietly.

"Yeah," I said, catching my breath. "I'm fine. I'm just going to . . . get ready for bed."

"Okay." Lorna picked up her blankets and went after Missy.

I closed the door and rechecked everything, just to be safe. The bathroom, the closets, under the beds. Nothing seemed amiss. I took a deep breath and tossed my coat on the hook behind the door. Then I turned to my dresser for my pajamas and froze.

No. Couldn't go in there. No drawers.

Rationally, I knew that all I had seen were the moving curtains, but I was irrationally scared anyway. I pulled my sweater off over my head and glanced at the closet.

No. Couldn't go in there either.

Feeling childish, I folded my sweater and placed it atop my closed laptop. Suddenly, I felt exhausted. Beaten down by my own paranoia. I didn't want to wash my face or brush my teeth or check my e-mail or do anything. My bag for tomorrow was already packed, sitting on the floor at the end of my bed. If I went to sleep, I could wake up and go to New York. Get out of here and not see this room for two whole days. Two whole days in a place that didn't know me. Two whole days in a town where Cheyenne's memory couldn't haunt me. Two whole days where whoever was messing with me couldn't reach me.

New York. The words were like a promise. I would feel less crazy there. I knew I would.

Jeans and T-shirt still on, I crawled under the covers and, leaving the overhead light blazing, attempted to get some sleep.

POWER TRIP

The lobby of the exclusive Gramercy Park Hotel was like something out of a modern-goth *Alice in Wonderland*, with its checkerboard floors, abstract art, ornate chandeliers, and dark stone walls. Yet it was somehow cozy. Comfortable. Welcoming.

In two words it was this:

Not Billings.

I felt myself start to breathe easier as we stepped further inside. There was a couple at the front desk surrounded by piles of buttery leather luggage, a tiny dog peeking out from the woman's handbag. A group of men in tailored suits strode by us in heated conversation, clearly on their way to some high-powered brunch, and they all stopped talking to check us out as they went by. One even surreptitiously snapped our picture with his phone, which London and Vienna automatically posed for. This was not the kind of clientele one might find at the Super 8 in Croton. This place oozed glamour.

I wondered what our suite would be like. Imagined a sumptuous bed I could sink into and sleep in for real. For hours and hours and hours without dreams. I shook my head. I had a long day ahead of me in the most exciting city in the world, and suddenly, all I wanted to do was go to bed.

"Miss Simmons, Miss Clarke, good to see you again," the bellboy—who was way too cute to be a bellboy—greeted them as he loaded our bags onto a cart. "I'll take this up to your suite. Is there anything else I can get for you?"

London looked at the rest of us expectantly. "Should we lunch out, or have them bring something to our room?"

"Lunch? It's ten-thirty in the morning," I pointed out. "And we have appointments to keep."

"So we'll do brunch," Vienna said, sinking into a red velvet chaise. She leaned back and kicked her heels off. "God, it's so good to be home."

"Home? But you don't live here." Sabine said it like a question, glancing around almost warily. Apparently, she didn't feel as comfortable here as I did.

London and Vienna laughed. So did the bellboy. "Practically," they said in unison.

"You can take our things up," Noelle told the bellboy, handing him a few crisp bills from her Louis Vuitton wallet. "We'll let you know if we need anything else."

As the bellboy silently disappeared, Noelle sat down on the chaise near Vienna's feet and slid her arms out of her coat. "I say we head up to Sarabeth's for brunch, then hit Bloomingdale's and Dylan's. I'm definitely going to need chocolate later."

"Omigod, totally!" London squealed, perching on the edge of a round-backed love seat. "And Sarabeth's has that French toast with the—"

"You guys, we can't go out for brunch right now," I said, hovering with Sabine as the three of them got comfy. "We have an appointment to see the Regent in half an hour, then another at the studio at eleven-fifteen. I blocked out time for lunch at twelve-thirty."

"What are you, auditioning to be a cruise director?" Vienna joked, checking out a sunglassed couple as they walked by to see if they were anyone worth seeing.

"Yeah, Reed, why don't you just relax?" Noelle suggested. "This is a vacation. And besides, I went to a wedding at the Regent last year, and they tried to pass off this crap caviar from Maine or some god-awful place as something decadent. People were spitting it out into their napkins all night."

She, London, and Vienna all snickered like they were in on some inside joke, which just made me feel uncomfortable. Sabine as well, if I was reading her closed-off body language correctly. There was no way I was going to let Noelle completely hijack this weekend. I needed her input, definitely, but she wasn't going to tell me how to run this whole thing

"You guys, this is *not* a vacation," I said pointedly. "We're here to plan a fund-raiser to save Billings, remember? And I don't care about the caviar, because I wasn't planning on serving any anyway. So get your butts in gear. We've got appointments to keep."

Vienna and London looked at each other, and Vienna pushed herself up in her chaise, rolling her eyes. "God, Reed. You sound like my mother," she said. But she grabbed her black cashmere coat and stood.

"As long as we get to Dylan's at some point today, I'm happy," London said with a shrug. "Now that you brought it up, I can't stop thinking about their cappuccino gelato. Dee-*vine*."

Noelle eyed me as the Twin Cities buttoned their coats and smoothed their hair. I knew she couldn't believe she'd just been unceremoniously snubbed, and I felt a quick rush of triumph. I was in charge now. She was just going to have to get used to it.

With a heavy sigh, Noelle finally arose and picked up her coat. "All right, then. We'll go. But it is an utter waste of time."

"We'll call up the car!" London announced, grabbing Vienna's arm as they traipsed off toward the front desk.

Noelle slowly belted her black coat and looked at me with narrow-eyed interest. "You really are enjoying this power trip you're on, aren't you, Glass-Licker?"

"Just doing my job," I said with a forced smile.

She smirked and strolled off after the Twin Cities, leaving me alone for the moment with Sabine. Her brows knit as she adjusted her new, very trendy white cloche hat.

"Why does she call you Glass-Licker?" she asked.

I paused, letting the memory of my first-ever conversation with Noelle wash over me for a moment. Letting myself relish the fact that even though she couldn't give up the nickname, our positions in life had completely changed. So much so that the insulting moniker was starting to feel like a joke. An homage to times gone by. A term of endearment. Somehow, it didn't hold the same power it used to.

"It's a long story," I told Sabine, looping my arm through hers the way London and Vienna were always doing. "A long, stupid story."

SO FAR, SO PERFECT

"Oh my God, Vienna! I thought Etienne was going to *die* when he realized you let someone else trim your bangs!" London cried as we stepped out of the Lange family's chauffeured limo somewhere on West Thirteenth Street. A stiff wind nearly blew me off my feet, and a pair of NYU boys eyed us with interest as they strolled by.

"I think he actually cried. I swear I saw a tear," I added.

"Well, that's what he gets for refusing to come up to Easton every week to shape me," Vienna said blithely, flicking her hair away from her face. "I even offered to pay for his transportation, but no. He simply cannot be away from the city for an entire afternoon," she added, putting on Etienne's thick French accent. "It would mean *disastre!*"

We all laughed, slightly high on the triumphs of the morning. Not only had the proprietor at Tassos's studio of choice practically bent over backward to accommodate us once we'd dropped the photographer's name, but Vienna had guilted the owner of her salon into canceling all his appointments for next Saturday afternoon so that we could rent out the entire facility. We'd even had a chance to swing by Dylan's Candy Bar to load up on sugar. So far I'd consumed almost half a pound of gummy bears and a Wonka Bar. I was having actual fun, and had hardly thought of Josh or Cheyenne or Ivy all day. So far, so perfect.

"He should know better," Noelle sniffed as she looked up and down the sidewalk, trying to pinpoint our destination. "You and your sister have been his most loyal clients ever since you first sprouted hair."

"I forgot you had a sister," Sabine said to Vienna, hugging herself against the cold. "Will we get to meet her at the fund-raiser?"

"Are you kidding? She practically peed in her pants when I told her about Frederica Falk and the photo shoot. She already sent me her donation," Vienna said.

"What about your sister, Sabine? Did you invite her?" I asked.

"She's out of the country right now," Sabine replied, her face brightening at the subject. "But she so wishes she could come. I think she—"

"Where *is* this place?" Noelle asked, interrupting Sabine. Quite rudely, I thought. "I can never remember which entrance . . ."

Suddenly, a plain black door right in front of us opened and out stepped the single most perfect specimen of manhood I had ever laid eyes on outside a movie theater. He was tall, with highlighted blond hair, golden stubble all along his cut cheekbones, and blue eyes that could cut steel. His suit was black, his shirt a pristine, crisp white that was opened one extra button to show the top of his tanned chest. For a moment none of us breathed.

"Reed Brennan?" he asked with an inquisitive smile.

London had to forcibly shove me forward. "That would be me," I said to the supermodel.

His smile widened and he opened the door further. "Welcome to Suite 13."

"I don't care where we have this thing, we're hiring this guy as our doorman," I whispered to my friends.

"I second that!" Vienna offered.

Giggling like girls at a tea party, we hustled inside.

"I'm Lucas, the assistant manager of Suite 13," Mr. Hot said as he led us down a dimly lit hallway with red-glass lamps hanging from the ceiling. He offered me his hand to shake. It was warm, strong, and very large. "Here at the suite, we pride ourselves on being one of the most versatile spaces in all of Manhattan. With our high ceilings, moveable booths, and huge square footage, we can turn our suite into anything your heart desires."

We came out onto a balcony with two staircases on either side, descending at a curve to a large, pitlike room. There were huge bars on either side, and round, suede booths in dark jewel tones dotted the room, surrounding a gleaming black dance floor. I could just imagine the place decorated with dark floral centerpieces and swags of cloth, flashbulbs popping, and champagne flowing. It was incredible.

"Oh, no," Noelle said under her breath.

"Yeah. I know," Vienna replied. "Not good."

"What's going on?" I asked.

"Is there a problem?" Lucas added, gripping the railing with one hand.

"No. Not at all," Noelle replied smoothly, tossing her hair over her shoulders. "I just need to confer with my friends for a moment."

"Take your time," Lucas replied.

He moved a few feet off and whipped out his Treo. Noelle tugged my arm, leading all four of us into the tiny alcove outside the bathrooms.

"We can't have it here," she whispered.

"Why not? I like it," I replied.

"Dash had his seventeenth birthday party here," Noelle said, glancing over her shoulder. "I forgot about it until I saw the room."

My shoulder muscles coiled at the mere mention of Dash's name. At the not-so-new but still annoying realization that he and Noelle and everyone at Easton had had very full lives before I ever showed up there. That he and Noelle had a shared history I would never be a part of. I knew that hooking up with Dash had been wrong, but it still stung that he had been able to dismiss me so easily, without so much as a phone call or an explanation. All of this hit me from every angle as I stood there with Noelle, Sabine, and the Twin Cities waiting for my comment.

"So?" I said finally. "That was almost two years ago."

"Exactly," Sabine added, taking my side as always. "And you heard what Lucas said. The room can be anything we want it to be. We can make it look completely different."

Noelle smirked and glanced over at Vienna, who hid a laugh behind her hand. London simply chuckled out loud. Clearly, they were all so very amused at our naiveté. Which, of course, made my blood boil.

"First of all, it doesn't matter what Mr. Universe over there says—people will know it's the same place," Noelle replied in a facetious tone. "This is supposed to be the event of the season. You don't want it to feel as if it's been done before, do you?"

"You really don't," Vienna put in with a shudder.

"Like, really," London added helpfully.

I looked at Sabine, who suddenly seemed as uncertain as I felt. These people were, after all, the experts. And we still had four more places to see. One of them had to be as good. Still, I hated kowtowing to Noelle. Especially with the sting of Dash's name still searing my skin. But what else could I do?

"Fine," I said through my teeth. "Let's just go."

As we said goodbye to an understandably confused Lucas (I think he'd noticed our collective drool), I realized that even this far away from Easton, I wasn't completely free of my drama. Until Noelle had mentioned his name, I had forgotten that Dash was supposed to be in the city this weekend. That he and Noelle were supposed to have dinner with his parents.

Would he pick her up at our room? Would tonight be the first night I laid eyes on Dash McCafferty since the Legacy—the night he'd laid his eyes all over me?

So much for my focus.

Noelle couldn't stop checking out her own ass. As soon as we'd returned to the suite at the hotel, she'd taken a shower and then come out wearing a black dress that looked staid and conservative from the front with its high neckline, but had such a low-cut back that you could practically see the top of her butt crack. For the past fifteen minutes she'd been standing with her back to the mirror, craning her neck so that she could study the effect.

"Dash is a butt man," she explained. "You'd think he'd be a boob man, but he's totally not."

She finally turned around to smooth her hair. As I sat on the edge of my double bed, all I wanted to do was grab a chunk of her brown locks and tear. She had been talking about nothing but Dash for the past hour. About how he had booked them a separate room in the hotel so they could be alone later. About how it had been so long since they'd been together that he wasn't going to be able to keep his hands off of her. It all made me so vilely ill I was growing belligerent. I wanted Josh, not Dash. I did. But I was so sick of hearing about how much Dash wanted Noelle. So sick.

"Why would you think he'd be a boob man?" London asked, clicking off her cell phone. She looked down at her own mega-breasts, as if assessing whether they could ever grab Dash's attention. Vienna was in the corner, trying to wheedle free champagne for the photo shoot out of some vendor who'd done her mother's third wedding.

"Look at his father," Noelle said. "He may act all proper and upright all the time, but he's had *several* mistresses over the years and every one of them? Double-D's. At least."

Now I had to glance down at my own flattish chest. The fact that Dash had been attracted to me at all did kind of prove he was a butt guy. But of course, I couldn't weigh in.

"So you think sexual preference runs in the family?" Sabine asked, holding a dress up to herself as she looked in the smaller of our two mirrors. "Like it's genetic?"

Noelle rolled her eyes. "I wasn't trying to be scientific, Frenchie. I was just talking."

Sabine blushed and went into the bathroom to change her clothes. Yet another of Noelle's pointless jabs had hit home. What was her damage?

"So, I really think we should go with Loft Blanc," Noelle said, grabbing her lip gloss and leaning toward the mirror. "It's the hottest new venue in town. People will be beyond impressed if they see it on the invite."

Loft Blanc was this admittedly amazing space in the Meatpacking

District with high ceilings, huge windows overlooking the Hudson, and an incredible collection of modern art adorning its otherwise stark walls. It also had outdoor, rooftop space, but considering I was 0 for 2 with rooftops in the past year, that wasn't much of a selling point for me. Besides, it was November. Who wanted to mingle on a rooftop in New York in November?

"We've already been through this. There's no way we're having it there," I told her, getting up and whipping my navy blue dress out of the closet. "Move on already."

Noelle paused with her lip gloss wand on her bottom lip. She shot me an annoyed look in the mirror, then slowly closed the tube, put it down, and turned to face me.

"Okay, that's it," she snapped, crossing her arms over her chest. In the mirror, her dress shifted enough so that I actually *could* see her butt crack. If Dash's mother was anywhere near as uptight as her reputation indicated, she was just going to *love* that dress. "What is your problem today?"

"I don't have a problem," I said, yanking my sweater off over my head. "You're the one with the problem. We're supposed to be making money on this thing, remember? Raising five million dollars? We can't spend five million if we want to make five million."

I shoved my jeans to the floor and stepped into the dress, zipping it up the side. Then I went over to the full-length mirror, subtly nudging Noelle aside, and started brushing through my hair like I was trying to bald myself. Sabine returned from the bathroom, looking simply elegant in a dark gray sheath.

"Everything okay?" she asked me.

"Fine," I said through my teeth.

"Reed, I thought I was here to help you make the right decision. I think we can all agree I know more about these things than you do." Noelle walked over to her dresser and selected a pair of diamond earrings from her small Hervé Léger bag.

"You don't have to insult her," Sabine said, irked.

"I wasn't. I was merely stating a fact," Noelle replied.

Sabine squared her shoulders and turned toward Noelle. "It sounded like an insult to me."

And to me. But I didn't say so. London got up and quietly slipped from the room, while Vienna continued to battle it out on the phone, oblivious to the rising tension.

"Reed, haven't you ever heard that old adage, 'You have to spend money to make money'?" Noelle asked, ignoring Sabine and training her attention on me. "Or is there so little cash where you come from, the phrase never happened to trickle down?"

"See! Another insult!" Sabine pointed out, lifting her hand.

My face was burning at this point, but I was used to that. I was used to Noelle's barbs. I knew they didn't really mean anything. It was just her way. Still, the fact that Sabine was so offended on my behalf made them sting a bit more than usual. "We don't have any money to spend, Noelle," I said, dropping my brush on the vanity with a clatter. "I say we go with the St. Sebastian. It was a beautiful space and much more traditional. The older alumni will appreciate it."

The St. Sebastian was this ancient, converted church with an arcing ceiling and beautiful stained glass windows looking down from above. When the proprietor showed us photos of the many ways they had transformed the space for weddings, album launches, and fund-raisers, I was sold. Plus it was reasonable. As reasonable as one could get in NYC. Noelle, of course, thought it had been done.

"Fine. We'll do it your way," Noelle said. She spritzed a cloud of perfume, then stepped through it. "But we're going to spend more money dressing that place up than we would if we simply went with Loft Blanc."

At that moment the doorbell to our suite rang. My heart all but stopped.

"I'll get it!" London shouted from her bedroom on the opposite side of the sunken living room.

"Dash is here," Noelle said, grabbing her clutch purse and a sheer silver cardigan off the vanity. "We can talk more about this later."

Dash was here. Dash was here. Dash was here. The moment Noelle was out of the room, I double-checked my hair and gave myself a quick powder, blush, and lip gloss makeover.

"Finally I get to meet the famous Dash McCafferty. Is he as big a bitch as his girlfriend?" Sabine asked.

I rolled my eyes, shoved my feet into my shoes, and walked unsteadily out to the living area of our suite, my ankles teetering thanks to the thick carpet and my nerves. Noelle was halfway to the door. London was just about to open it. Vienna came tearing out of my room behind me, phone closed now, and rushed to London's side, all smiles.

What the heck were those two up to? Not that I cared much at the moment. All I could think was that Dash was behind that door. What would he say to me? What would I say to him? Would Noelle be able to tell what had happened between us?

London whipped open the door and everyone froze. The guy standing on the threshold was not Dash McCafferty. He was, in fact, Dash's physical opposite. Tall, sure, but tan. Dark. Lean. With long black hair that just skimmed the bottom of his earlobes.

Dominic Infante. Dominic Infante and a single purple orchid in a white ceramic pot.

He glanced around at each of us, dotted as we were around the room, and stopped on me.

"Reed. You look lovely," he said, holding out the orchid.

Whahuh?

"Look what we imported just for you!" London announced.

She and Vienna flanked the door like a pair of game-show models showing off the latest prize. Noelle glanced back at me over her shoulder, amused.

"Guess someone else has a date tonight," Noelle said.

Realizing it was my turn to speak, I took a few steps forward. "You came all the way down here from school just for me?" I asked Dominic.

He looked me up and down, his eyes lingering on my legs, my hips, my chest, and then my face. "Wouldn't you?"

My heart actually fluttered.

"Damn. Good answer," Noelle said behind me.

Dominic handed the potted orchid to me, and London whisked it right out of my hands.

"Shall we?" Dominic said, stepping aside to make room in the doorway.

I looked at London and Vienna and their insane Cheshire grins and knew there was no way I could turn this down. Not without a fight. And why would I want to? Why not get out of here before the torture of seeing Dash and Noelle together could occur? Why not hit New York with a gorgeous Italian maybe-prince? This weekend was supposed to be about distraction. About getting away. I could think of no better method of escape.

I smiled and grabbed my coat. "I guess we shall."

PART OF THE FAMILY

"This place is incredible," I said to Dominic, laying my long, flat menu aside.

When we had arrived at the small restaurant, tucked away in the West Village, it hadn't looked like much. Just a brick basement in someone's brownstone. But once inside, we had been ushered through the small, cozy dining area and out onto this even cozier patio, where only a dozen intimate tables were placed among the trees that grew right out of the brick beneath our feet. There were heat lamps placed around the periphery to ward off the November chill, and white twinkle lights were strung from the tree branches overhead. I couldn't believe places like this existed in Manhattan.

"I'll tell my cousin you said so," Dominic replied.

"Your cousin?"

"Yes. My cousin Antony owns this place," Dominic said casually. His accent really was alluring. "There is usually a long wait list to get in, but when I told him of your beauty, he managed to clear a table for us."

I blushed as I looked across the tiny table at him. Dominic had been saying things like this ever since we left the hotel, but I couldn't tell if he was serious, or if he was just feeding me lines. But then, what did it matter? I could use the ego boost either way.

"I was thinking that after this I might take you to a couple of my usual places," Dominic said, placing his menu down.

"Usual places?" I asked.

"Clubs. Have you done the club scene?" he asked.

"Um, no," I replied. "And I'm not really sure I should. I have to get up kind of early in the morning."

"Well, you could always just stay up all night," Dominic replied with a smile. A suggestive smile? "That's what I usually do."

"We'll see," I replied. Time for a subject change. I didn't want to know what he thought we would do if we stayed up together all night. "So, is your cousin here? I'd love to meet him."

"He promised to bring out his special dessert for us personally." Dominic took a sip of his white wine and smiled. "If we make it through the first four courses. The service here is truly Italian. Which means excessive."

My stomach grumbled as a delicious-looking dish was carried past our table.

"Sounds good to me. I'm starving," I replied.

Dominic smiled. "A girl with an appetite. Are you sure you go to Easton?"

I laughed and felt myself truly start to relax for the first time all night. Suddenly I felt grateful to London and Vienna for blindsiding me with this date. If I had gone out for dinner with the two of them and Sabine, I was sure the conversation would have centered around the fund-raiser and maybe even Cheyenne. Maybe they would even have gotten around to asking me what happened with Josh. But here I was simply being showered with compliments and attention. A much more satisfying way to spend an evening.

"Actually, you'd be surprised by how much the girls in Billings can put away," I told him. "Just a couple of days ago we—"

My cute little anecdote died on my tongue as I heard familiar voices just on the other side of the patio door. I had about half a second to prepare before Noelle stepped out into the courtyard, with Dash's hand on her waist. I felt as if the bricks were falling away beneath the legs of my chair. So much so that I actually gripped my armrests for support.

Dash. Dash's lips, Dash's hands, Dash's eyes, Dash's longing desperation. Suddenly every image, every feeling, everything from the night of the Legacy came rushing back, hitting me like a tidal wave to the chest. Dominic and I had scored the back corner table, and in the dim light Noelle had yet to spot us, but Dash had. He had looked right into my eyes the second he arrived, as if he had expected me to be there. But then he tripped. He braced himself on one of the tree trunks to keep from going down.

My heart was in my throat. Okay. So maybe he hadn't entirely forgotten that night.

"Dash! Are you all right?" his mother asked. She could only be his mother. Tall. Blond. Perfectly manicured and coiffed. Then his father, the spitting image of Dash, but with salt-and-pepper hair.

"Just a couple of days ago you . . . ?" Dominic prodded, unaware that anything was amiss.

Noelle finally figured out where Dash was looking and spotted me. I endeavored to smile. She whispered something to Dash's parents and they all looked over. Dash cleared his throat about ten times and straightened his tie. Finally, at the obvious prodding of his mother, he cleared it one last time, squared his shoulders, and walked over to us.

Omigod. Omigod, omigod, omigod.

"Is something wrong?" Dominic asked.

"Dash," I said through my teeth.

"What?"

"Dash McCafferty is here," I said.

Dominic looked up just as Dash arrived at our table.

"Reed. Dom. How are you guys?" Dash asked, his tone formal.

"McCafferty!" Dominic cheered, getting up to hug his former dorm mate. "How are you? How is everything at Yale?"

Thank God Dominic knew him. If I had been forced to speak first, I might have thrown up on Dash's extremely buffed shoes. As the two of them briefly caught up, I stared at the underside of Dash's chiseled chin, a thousand questions flooding my mind.

Why haven't you called? What the hell happened that night? Why did you get back together with Noelle? When?

And why do you have to be So. Effing. Hot?

Not that I could have said any of those things with Dominic there and Noelle looking on. Not that I could have said any of those things without dying of mortification even if Dash and I had been alone.

"Reed," Dash said finally, turning toward me.

I looked up at him. My many queries must have been blatantly readable in my eyes, because I stopped him cold.

"I . . ." His jaw worked. "You look . . . I mean, it's been a while."

"Not that long," I heard myself say.

A pang of something crossed his face. Regret? Annoyance? It was impossible to tell. And then Noelle swooped in. Her coat had been removed, but she wore the light, open-weave cardigan over her dress, camouflaging her butt crack, apparently, until she could get Dash alone.

"Hundreds of restaurants in Manhattan and here you are!" she said gaily, taking Dash's hand. "What are the chances?"

"I'm glad you decided on this one," Dominic said politely. "You're in for a wonderful meal."

"Well. Let's get to it then," Noelle said. "You two have fun!" She practically dragged Dash away, but not before he was able to say one last thing over his shoulder. "See you guys at the fund-raiser."

And that was that.

Noelle and Dash joined his parents at their table in the opposite corner. Mercifully, the two of them sat with their backs to us or I would have never made it through the meal. Still, I couldn't help glancing over every now and then and noticing how comfortable

Noelle looked with his parents. Touching his dad's arm, making jokes with his mom. As if she was already part of the family.

Seeing Noelle and Dash together, I couldn't help but imagine what the rest of my night would be like. Best-case scenario? I returned to the suite and Noelle came back alone to gush about her dinner with the McCaffertys. Worst-case scenario? Tomorrow at brunch I'd hear about the hours Noelle and Dash had spent in their suite, sharing their mutual admiration for the female backside.

Ew.

"You know what, Dominic? I'm in," I said.

His eyebrows shot up. "For what?"

"The clubs," I said, reaching for my wine. "I'd love to check out your usual places."

UNDER THE INFLUENCE

Dominic danced with a champagne bottle gripped in one hand and the other hand locked around my waist. From the moment we stepped through the doors of Platinum—a place where nothing related to the name aside from the fact that everyone there was constantly whipping out their platinum credit cards to pay for insanely overpriced bottles of alcohol—he had not been without a bottle. Had he been working on the same one all night, or was this his second? It couldn't be his third. No one could consume that much without regurging. Although from the way his brown eyes swam in their sockets, I wouldn't have been totally shocked if that was the case.

"Having fun?" he asked, his face looming ever so close to mine. Even with that proximity, it was difficult to hear him over the deafening music.

"Absolutely!"

The DJ was amazing, after all. And the dancing was a release, as long as Dominic wasn't breathing in my face. Everywhere I looked I saw vaguely familiar faces. Models, rap artists, rock stars, young socialites. Champagne flowed, diamonds flashed, girls squealed and posed for pictures. I wondered how many of these moments would end up eternalized in the tabloids the next morning.

"Reed! I love this place!" Sabine shouted, throwing her arms around my neck from behind. She tugged me away from Dominic, and I felt as if I could breathe again. "Thanks for inviting us!"

"You're welcome!" I shouted.

The moment we left the restaurant I had speed-dialed Sabine and the Twin Cities, hoping they would (a) make this part of the night more fun, and (b) give me an excuse to avoid kissing Dominic and/or going back to wherever he was staying. From the way he'd been looking at me all night, I had a feeling he had one or both in mind. Thank God Platinum had turned out to be a Twin Cities–approved destination.

I turned around to dance with Sabine. Dominic moved right in behind me, grinding against my back. I tried to ignore the invasion.

"Where are London and Vienna?" I asked.

"They saw some guys they knew, so they're bringing them over," Sabine shouted in reply. She glanced over my shoulder at Dominic and made a disgusted face. I was feeling a little disgusted myself. "I'm taking her to the bathroom!" Sabine yelled at him. Then she grabbed my arm and pulled me away. I had never been more grateful.

"I will be here!" Dominic shouted after us.

We got to a less crowded corner of the dance floor and Sabine stopped. "Are you okay?"

"Yeah. Thank you for getting me out of there, though," I said, lean-ing toward her ear. "He was totally fine until he started drinking like a sponge. Now all of a sudden he's Mr. Inappropriate Touching."

"There you guys are!" London sang, holding Vienna's hand aloft as she wove toward us.

They both had full martini glasses, the liquid sloshing over the sides as they walked. The guys they had brought along looked like two Abercrombie models, one with dark skin and a white shirt, the other with light skin and a black shirt. Both ridiculously hot.

"Let's dance!" Vienna said, throwing her arm over my shoulder.

I glanced behind me, but couldn't spot Dominic in the crowd. Who cared where he was, anyway? A few minutes without his paws all over me felt like a good idea. Plus this place was so jam-packed there was a decent chance he'd never find us again. Might not be the most polite way in the world to end a date, but at least it would be easy. And this weekend I was all about easy.

"Don't worry about him," Sabine told me, clearly noticing that I was in crowd-scan mode. "I'm sure he's already molesting some other girl. Hopefully one who feels like being molested."

I laughed and decided to just live in the moment. And so I did. I danced with my friends, letting go of everything. Letting the music move through me. Letting it shove out all thoughts of the guys I wanted and the girls they apparently wanted instead of me. Letting thoughts of Billings and its possible closing and of the strange, Cheyenne-related happenings fade. I just let it all go and had fun with my friends. Even-tually white-shirted Abercrombie boy moved from Vienna to me and we danced together for a good half hour. Unlike Dominic, any touching he did was appropriate. He had incredible rhythm and an even more incredible smile.

Hmmm. Maybe the next boyfriend of the Billings president could be a wild card. Someone from outside Easton's walls . . .

Now all I had to do was find out who the heck he was.

"What's your name?" I shouted, leaning toward him.

"Fine!" he replied, smiling and nodding to the beat.

Yeah. Communication was not so easy inside Platinum. Whatever. I decided to let it go and just dance. Which was what I was doing when I felt a hand on my shoulder. I turned around and had to peel my hair from my sweaty cheeks. Dominic stood in front of me, his face gleaming, the champagne bottle still in hand.

"You never came back from the bathroom," he said.

"I couldn't find you," I lied.

He grinned. "Well, good that I found you, then." He took a slug from the bottle, then offered it to me. "Drink?" he asked me for about the millionth time that night.

"No, thanks." I wrinkled my nose. I had already downed one glass of wine at the restaurant and I did not want to get drunk. I had learned my lesson at the Legacy and the day after. Being hungover again was not in my immediate plans.

"You have had nothing to drink since we got here," he accused.

"So?" I replied.

"So you should lighten up. Look around. It's a party." He spread his arms wide and clunked a Hollywood starlet in the head with his bottle.

"Hey! Watch it!" she shouted, shoving him.

Dominic merely laughed.

"I know it's a party, and I'm having fun," I shouted at him. I glanced back at Abercrombie boy, but he had moved on to some chick in a pink wig, damn it. "I don't need to drink to have fun!" I told Dominic.

Dominic snorted a laugh, wavering slightly in place, then took another slug from the bottle. "Cheyenne was right about you," he said.

My blood seemed to freeze in my veins. I looked over my shoulder at Sabine and the Twin Cities. Apparently they had heard it too, because they had all stopped dancing.

"Excuse me?" I said.

"She was always saying how you had this stick up your butt. Which made sense, since you were from the sticks," he said with another snort.

"Shut it, Infante!" Vienna snapped, coming over to stand next to me. London and Sabine gathered around as well. "Just because you're a pseudo prince doesn't mean you can talk to my girl like that."

Dominic sniffed and took another drink.

"Wait. You and Cheyenne talked about me?" I demanded, my heart pounding a mile a minute. "When? Why?"

"Cheyenne was an old friend," he said. "A very *close* friend," he added suggestively. "She liked to cuddle afterward. And talk."

Vienna and I looked at one another, skeeved.

"*You* hooked up with Cheyenne? When?" Vienna demanded.

"All the time," Dominic replied, standing up straight. "Girl really made her way through Ketlar. But Hollis was her ultimate conquest, and now I can see why he went for her, even though he was with you. Cheyenne was hot behind closed doors. But you . . ." He looked me up and down with disdain, a complete one-eighty from the way he'd checked me out at our hotel suite. "You are kind of a frigid bitch, aren't you?"

I felt as if all the wind had just been knocked out of me. I wanted to slap him, but before I could regain my senses, London did it for me. And Dominic was so drunk, he went down like a house of cards right there in the middle of the dance floor.

"Ow. That hurt," London said, pouting as she shook her hand.

"Wow, London. Thanks," I replied.

"Come on. Let's get out of here," Sabine said, putting her arm around me.

"I don't get it," I said as we shoved our way through the crowd of curious onlookers who were now surrounding Dominic. "He was so nice earlier."

"Bad drunk," Vienna theorized, giving me a squeeze from the opposite side. "I'm sure he didn't mean any of that."

"Right."

She had a point. I knew from experience that people could turn into monsters when they were under the influence. Look at Thomas. My mother. Even me. Would I have hooked up with Dash that night if it hadn't been for all those drinks? I hoped not. I hoped that my sober self was better than that.

"So. Guess we're scratching Dominic off the list," Vienna said, placing our coat-check tags down at the counter near the front of the club. "Unless you can keep him sober."

"Not likely," I replied, forcing a laugh. Besides, I wasn't sure I would ever be able to forget the things he'd just said, drunk or not. Dominic might have been the perfect arm candy of a Billings president on the surface, but he was clearly not for me. Besides, I didn't want any of Cheyenne Martin's sloppy seconds, which apparently meant most of Ketlar was off the table.

It was amazing how these boys kept reinforcing what a catch Josh had been. Amazing and really, really annoying.

The moment we walked through the doors of Barneys New York the next morning, the Twin Cities took off like a pair of sugar addicts who'd just been let loose at a chocolate factory. I glanced at Noelle and Sabine and laughed.

"Looks like we're on our own."

Now please just don't kill each other.

That morning over an early brunch, we called the St. Sebastian and booked it for the fund-raiser dinner and auction. Noelle hadn't been all that happy about it, but she had agreed with me in the end. Then we had called Kiki and Astrid to give them the dates and told them to send out the e-mail invites ASAP. Now, everything in place, it was time for a little retail therapy. The Billings Girls' therapy of choice.

We strolled through the main floor with its wide walkways and gleaming glass counters, and then down the stairs to the beauty department. Noelle wandered off toward the makeup counters to check out a few things, and I was hit with a whiff of perfume. I paused and looked over at an anorexic-looking woman dressed in a form-fitting black suit who was offering samples of some new scent. The cash I'd been given by the Billings alumni was currently burning a hole in my Chloé bag, and I had never bought myself perfume before. Could I possibly spend my green on something so decadent?

Why not? This was my weekend of freedom. I could do whatever I wanted.

"I'm going to go try out some perfume," I told Sabine.

"I'll come with you," she replied.

As if I ever thought she was going to go after Noelle.

After assaulting my senses with fifteen ridiculously strong scents, I chose a clean, invigorating perfume called, appropriately, Free, and barely broke a sweat handing over the many bills I need to shell out for the tiny bottle. The moment the transaction was done, my iPhone rang, and Vienna's picture came up.

"What's up?" I asked. "Max out your credit already?"

She ignored my joke. "Where are you bitches? We're trying on dresses. Get your butts up here!" she shouted.

"Guess we're going to try on dresses," I told Sabine and Noelle, who had just joined us with a small bag from La Mer.

"Sounds like a plan," she said. She glanced at my bag.

"I can't believe I'm actually in Barneys," Sabine breathed, looking around as we ascended the escalator.

I glanced at Noelle, knowing some obnoxious comment was right on the tip of her tongue. She caught my look, and instead of saying whatever she wanted to say, she looked away. Huh. Maybe Noelle was starting to get bored of teasing Sabine. Or maybe whatever she and Dash had done last night had left her in such a good mood that her heart wasn't in it. She hadn't returned to our suite until this morning.

Clench.

Okay. Not thinking about that.

We found London and Vienna in the spacious dressing room off the couture section on five, being waited on by two very eager assistants. From the looks of their rooms, they had already tried on several dresses and sorted them into racks of "yes's" and "no's."

"Oooh! What'd you get?" London asked, grabbing at me and Noelle and our little Barneys bags.

"Perfume," I said, as she pulled out the bottle so she and Vienna could inspect it.

Vienna spritzed it and smiled. "Nice. Very bold. Very you."

"Thanks," I said, beaming as I reclaimed the expensive bottle. They seemed much less interested in Noelle's face cream. "Have you guys found anything yet?"

"We found something for *you*!" London announced, shoving a gold minidress at me. "You have to try this one on! With your legs and butt, the guys will go catatonic when they see you."

At the mention of my butt I froze. I saw Noelle check it out in the mirror. Was she thinking of Dash? Wondering if he'd ever noticed it? Wondering if she'd been wrong about our flirtation being so very innocent?

"She's right. You'll look hot in that," Noelle said finally. She slipped out of her coat and glanced at one of the hovering workers. "Bring me something sophisticated and black. Only black," she told them.

"Right away, Miss Lange," the girl said. Of course she knew Noelle's name. "We have some fabulous new things you'll just adore."

"I'm sure I will," Noelle replied, taking a seat on the velvet chair in the corner.

And adore them she did, considering she bought five of them. After trying on practically everything in the store, London and Vienna went home with two new dresses each. I bought the gold one, which basically made me look runway-worthy. It put another dent in my cash, but it was totally worth it. Noelle kept urging me to use the Billings Alumni Fund instead, since the dress was for the fund-raiser, but I didn't feel right about it. Sabine, meanwhile, snapped up a Marc Jacobs on sale. Even though she came from money like the rest of the Billings Girls, her family had actually taught her frugality. Go figure.

Afterward, we hit the CO-OP on the top floor, where the Twin Cities stocked up on more pairs of jeans than any two people could ever wear in a lifetime, and I splurged on a funky BCBG sweater that cost more than my mother brought home each week from her new job at Target. I could get used to this having-money thing. Although the wad was rapidly dwindling at this point. Perhaps I'd receive a new stash at Christmas or something. I'd have to hold out hope.

By the time we returned to our waiting limo, we were so loaded down with bags, they didn't all fit in the trunk. We had to squeeze a few in between us on the seats. I let out a sigh as I dropped back against the cool leather, feeling tired, but in a very self-satisfied way.

"That was a productive weekend," Noelle said as the chauffeur closed the door behind us.

"Yeah, for American Express!" Vienna joked, shoving some bags into the corner near the partition.

"Back to Easton, then?" I said with a smile, happy to discover that I was actually looking forward to getting back there. This weekend really had been like a vacation. I felt so much more relaxed and happy. Like everything was going to be all right. That retail therapy always did the trick.

"Back to Easton," Noelle replied. "Drew! We're ready!" she shouted at her driver.

"Noelle, whip out those Prada boots you got again so I can drool over them," London said, scooting forward in her seat as Drew edged into traffic.

"If you insist," Noelle said smugly, pulling the box out.

London delicately lifted one of the black leather boots from the tissue inside the box and hugged it. "Omigod. I want to marry these boots!"

"I don't know why you didn't just get a pair for yourself," Noelle said.

London scowled and handed the coveted boot back. "I tried them on, but they pinched my feet."

"Of course they did, Ms. Big Foot. You totally need that surgery where they pare down your tootsies," Vienna said.

"Ew! Vienna!" I exclaimed.

"What? Her feet are as wide as a duck's. Seriously! Have you not noticed? Here! I'll show you!" Vienna exclaimed, grabbing one of London's legs and lifting it onto her lap. She tugged at the lace of one of London's Coach booties and tried to pry it off.

"Leave my monster feet alone!" London squealed, giggling as she tried to squirm from Vienna's grasp.

"No! The world needs to know about your deformity!" Vienna said with a faux cackle.

We were all laughing as Drew pulled the car out onto the FDR. Then, suddenly, all five of our phones beeped and sang in near unison. Everyone scrambled in their bags, but my phone was hidden somewhere at the bottom of my Chloé. Vienna was the first to unearth her cell.

"Omigod!" London and Vienna blurted in unison. They were both gaping down at Vienna's screen, looking ashen, London's legs still hooked over Vienna's.

"What?" I asked, sitting up straight again. "What's wrong?"

"The cops just dragged Ivy off for questioning!" London said, her eyes wide.

My heart started to pound. They had come for her. They had finally come for her.

"About Cheyenne?" Sabine asked, glancing at me with concern.

Vienna swallowed and nodded. "There must be new evidence or something. They've actually reopened the case as a possible murder."

Everything inside of me deflated. We sat there in stunned silence, letting the true meaning of this sink in. Possible murder. Another murder. There could very well be a killer somewhere on campus. Again. Even though I had known this was a possibility, I still felt as if I was hearing the news for the first time. I guess I had been hoping it would all just go away. Now that hope had been dashed.

I looked up at Noelle, my skin cold. She stared grimly back. We were going to have to go through this. Again.

GOING DOWN

Later that night Constance, Rose, Tiffany, and I walked into the solarium together. I hadn't seen the place so dead in months, not since Coffee Carma opened. But that night the place was so hushed it could have been a museum. People were talking—of course they were talking—but they were talking in whispers. Paranoid, frightened whispers.

It was all too familiar. Too eerily, skin-tinglingly familiar. Cheyenne's death was bad enough. But Cheyenne's possible murder? It had left the place grim. I wanted to tell them all what I knew—that Cheyenne's grieving parents had asked for the investigation and that the police weren't 100 percent behind it—but I couldn't. Not without everyone knowing that I had been the one to visit with the cops last week. I glanced right and saw Josh alone at a table with a book open in front of him. He was looking at me but quickly looked away. What did that mean?

"I really don't believe this is happening," Constance said under her breath, clinging to the sleeves of her white sweater. As we wove our way around the café tables and couches, every eye in the room was on us. The Billings Girls. Once again we were at the center of a murder investigation.

"How could it have been murder?" Tiffany whispered. "We were all there. We all saw her. She took pills. There was no violence, no struggle. She wrote a note. I don't understand."

Two notes, actually. But there was no need for them to know that.

"Well, clearly the police have something or they wouldn't be questioning all these people," Rose said. Her normally healthy skin looked waxy under her red ringlets. "I just can't imagine it. She must have been so scared. Why didn't she call for help? Why didn't she—"

Rose's voice broke and she covered her face with her sleeve, which was pulled down over her hand. Tiffany put her arm around her and shot me a sad look.

"We'll go get a table," she said.

My insides quaked as Constance and I joined the short line at the counter. I wanted to squirm to try to make this awful feeling go away, but I knew it wouldn't work. This feeling wasn't going anywhere anytime soon. No point in letting half the school see me fidgety and nervous and scared in the meantime.

"I hate this. I hate it," Constance said, hugging herself tighter. She leaned closer to me as the worker behind the counter fired up the foam maker. "Do you realize that someone in this room might have killed her? Might have snuck right into our dorm while we were all asleep and killed Cheyenne? I can't handle this."

I was about to respond when the already quiet vibe went deathly still. As if someone had just hit the mute button on the sound track of our lives. Startled by the sudden silence, I turned around. Ivy stood in the doorway, looking like a rabid pit bull ready to strike.

No one moved. They had let her go. The police had let her go. Her blue eyes found me in the crowd.

"You," she said under her breath.

She stormed across the room. Everyone turned to look at me now. To see what I would do. They must have been disappointed, because I could think of nothing. Like a deer in headlights, I just let her come.

"Ivy." Josh stood as she passed before him, but she flinched away. In two seconds her hand was on my arm. Grip like a vice. She dragged me away from Constance, who let out a gasp.

"What are you—"

"Back off," Ivy snapped at her.

Ivy pulled me into the corner near the emergency exit where we were partially hidden from view by a large potted plant. I couldn't see anyone from this vantage point, which meant they couldn't see me either. My pulse started to race. Suddenly the airy room was full of murmurs. What was Ivy doing? No one treated the president of Billings this way. The thought finally woke me up from my stunned stupor and I snatched my arm back, sure her grip was going to leave finger-shaped bruises.

"What is wrong with you, you—"

"I know you were in my room at the Legacy," Ivy said, cutting me off. She stepped right up in my face, her dark hair like two blankets around those eerie blue eyes. I took an instinctive step back, then hated myself for it. "You found my albums. You left them all over the floor, so I know that you know."

"Know what?" I said, stalling for time.

"Don't play dumb. It's beneath you," Ivy said.

Weird. Was that a compliment?

"Did you tell the police about me and Cheyenne?" she asked. She was all accusatory. Indignant. As if *I* had done something wrong. I lifted my chin and looked her dead in the eye.

"Yes, I did. You've got to admit, it's all a little suspect," I said firmly. "You guys are best friends all the way up through sophomore year, but now you hate each other out of nowhere? Put it all together with your shady criminal past and whatever this deal was with your grandmother and you start to look like a suspect to me."

"Shut up," Ivy said venomously. She didn't even register surprise at the revelation that I knew about her family and her indiscretions. "Do not talk about things you will never understand."

"So make me understand them," I replied, growing warm from all the adrenaline. "What the hell happened between you guys?"

"I don't have to explain myself," Ivy said with a sneer. "Least of all to you."

That sneer got right under my already taut skin.

"You think you're so superior, don't you? You people with your rituals and your sisterhood crap and your blackball ceremonies," Ivy said, her eyes narrowing. "Well, guess what, Reed? It's your turn now. Your turn to find out what it feels like to be blackballed. We're going to see how you like it."

I couldn't breathe. All I could see were those black marbles in my desk drawer. She had put them there. She had to have put them there. Why else would she be saying these things to me? Ivy was my stalker. She had somehow gotten her hands on a key to Billings, whether by stealing Kiki's or getting one in the office or finding one some other way—it didn't matter. However she had done it, she was guilty. There was no other explanation.

"I've never done anything to you," I said through my teeth, trembling from head to toe. "I barely even know you. Why are you doing this to me?"

Ivy smiled evilly. "Haven't done anything. Yet."

She turned to go and I instinctively reached out and grabbed her. "Stop lying, you freak."

Her eyes went wide as she looked at my fingers on her arm. "You little—"

"Ivy!"

Josh came up behind her and touched her shoulder just as she made a move to attack. To hit me, push me, scratch me? I had no idea. But the touch of his fingers stopped her.

"Come on," he said in her ear. Right in her ear. Their cheeks touching. Josh's skin against hers. I was going to throw up. "Come on. Let's get out of here," he said in that soothing voice I knew so well.

It sent shivers of regret and longing and pain down my spine. "You don't need this. Let's just go."

Ivy bent her head forward. Leaned her shoulder into him. "Fine. I'll go."

Josh turned away, his hand now on her back. He never looked at me. Not once.

"But this isn't over," Ivy said to me as he tugged her along. Said loud enough for every salivating student in the solarium to hear. "You just sealed it, Reed. Billings is going down. And I'm taking down every last one of you with it."

NOT HAPPENING

Ivy. It was her. I was sure of it now. She hated Billings. She hated me. Maybe she even had some sort of sick, twisted, leftover loyalty to Cheyenne. She was the one messing with me. She had to be.

As I walked back to Billings with my friends, my hands shoved deep inside my pockets, the cold air clearing out my senses, it all made perfect sense. Maybe Cheyenne was the one who had ended their friendship. If what Noelle had said was true—that Ivy had turned down the invite to Billings—then Cheyenne might very well have cut the girl off. Nothing meant more to her than Billings. She never would have been able to accept the fact that someone didn't want to be there as much as she did. So maybe Cheyenne had ended their friendship, but Ivy still loved her. Maybe Ivy felt as if Billings had been responsible for the end of her friendship, for the end of her best friend's life. And now . . . now she was taking it out on me.

"Reed? Reed, where are you right now?" Tiffany asked, leaning forward to get into my line of sight as we reached the front door.

"Just thinking," I replied. Oddly enough, I actually felt relieved. Happy. Safe. There was a theory that made sense. One that even exonerated all my friends. I couldn't believe that I had ever suspected any of them. Astrid, Shelby, even Missy. I hated Ivy for making me into a paranoid freak who thought her friends were plotting against her. But at the same time, I was ecstatic to know that I was safe among my friends. Everything was going to be fine.

"Don't waste any of your brain space on Ivy," Tiffany said, rolling her eyes. "The girl has completely lost it."

She yanked open the first door and used her electronic key to get through the second.

"You guys want to hang out for a while?" Rose asked as we all shed our coats in the foyer.

"Actually, I think I'm just going to go check my e-mail and go to bed," I replied. "It's been a long weekend."

I trudged up the stairs to my room, Constance and Sabine trailing behind me, gabbing about Ivy and whether she could possibly be a killer. I tried to tune them out, but they were far too loud.

"I never liked the girl. The way she walks around here acting like she runs the place," Sabine said.

"And she looks like a witch. With that pointy face and the dark hair and all the black clothes," Constance added. "Honestly? It's like *The Wizard of Oz*. Cheyenne was the good blond witch all in pink, and Ivy's the scary, psycho witch all in black."

Sabine paused for a moment. "But in that story, the good witch survived and the bad witch melted."

"Maybe we should go throw some water on her and see what happens," Constance said flatly as they followed me into our room.

As they continued to gab over on Sabine's side, I opened my computer with a sigh and brought up my e-mail. Instantly, my heart stopped beating. I had an e-mail from Dash. Right there at the top of the page. It was titled "Long overdue," and it had been sent from a new e-mail address. Apparently he had wised up about his girl-friend's e-mail know-how.

Finally. Finally something. The guy sure took his dear, sweet time. I glanced over my shoulder to make sure the girls were occupied, then started to sit down in my chair. I was about halfway to seated, when the chair and the whole world dropped out from under me.

Right beneath Dash's e-mail was an e-mail from Cheyenne. And beneath that another. And beneath that another. I shakily reached for the mouse and scrolled down. Her name filled the whole page. It filled the entire page after that. And another. And another. The more I clicked, the more my eyes stung, watering until I couldn't focus anymore.

I had blocked Cheyenne's address. Changed my own. I had stopped this. How had these e-mails gotten through. How? Was it Ivy? Was she some kind of computer hacker? Was she trying to show me that she could get to me no matter where I was? A bubble rose up in my throat and before I could stop it, a strangled sound came right out. I slapped my hand over my mouth, shut the browser, and quickly powered down the computer. But it was too late. Sabine and Constance had stopped talking.

"Reed? Are you all right?"

"M'just . . . sick," I mumbled. And it was true. The second I spoke I felt dinner coming back up. I raced past them into the bathroom, slammed the door, and fell to my knees in front of the toilet. After retching for what felt like an eternity, I flushed and put my butt on the floor, shoving myself back against the wall, wondering if I'd ever really feel safe again.

SNAFU

The morning was always better. By the light of day everything seemed fine. Nightmares seemed impossible. Still, I didn't go near my computer. As much as I wanted to know what Dash's e-mail was all about, I couldn't handle Cheyenne's name staring me in the face like that. That was no way to start a day.

At breakfast everyone was discussing the upcoming fund-raiser, whom they might bring as dates, what they were going to wear, where they would stay in the city that night, when Portia came whirling in with a copy of the *New York Post*.

"O. M. G.!" she said dramatically, whipping the paper open and slapping it down in front of me. "Look at this!"

It was the infamous Page Six gossip column, and staring out at me was a large, full-color photo of Kiran Hayes in a hot pink dress, draped all over some Adonis and smiling seductively at the camera.

She had grown her dark hair out, and it fell in perfect waves over her tan shoulders and back. Gorgeous as always.

"What is this?" I asked, pulling it closer as Noelle, Tiffany, and Astrid rose out of their seats to better see.

"Check the cap!" Portia instructed, pointing a manicured nail at the text beneath.

"'International It Girl Kiran Hayes celebrates her eighteenth birthday in style at the Ritz in Amsterdam,'" I read aloud. "'But don't fret, kiddies. Word is Miss Hayes will be bringing the party stateside next month. Think you're a VIP? You'll know if you receive an invite.'"

"Sweet!" Tiffany said, sitting down again. "There's nothing like one of Kiran's birthday parties."

"She didn't have one last year," I pointed out.

"That was because of all the . . . unpleasantness," Noelle said dismissively.

"Did you guys know she was planning a party here?" Vienna asked from the other end of the table.

"No," I replied.

"Of course," Noelle said at the same time, digging out a spoonful of yogurt and berries from her bowl.

She looked at me from across the table and smirked. Of course she knew and I didn't. Of course. But did that mean I wasn't going to be invited? That I didn't rate as one of Kiran's VIPs?

"So, Reed. Have you thought about who *you're* going to bring to the fund-raiser?" Noelle asked, smoothly changing the subject as she took another bite of breakfast.

"Do I really need a date?" I asked. "I'm going to be busy enough as it is without babysitting some guy."

"Are you kidding? Of course you need a date," Portia said as she slid into a chair at the other end of the table. "How would it look if the chairwoman of the event didn't have a date? Answer? N.G."

Great. I had no idea people cared about such things. I glanced over at a small table near the corner, where Josh and Ivy sat together and alone, talking urgently over their untouched meals. Suddenly I felt hollow inside. Were the rumors that Josh and Ivy were together true, or did it just *look* that way? Part of me wished I knew for sure, but a larger part of me wanted to know nothing—wanted to be able to keep living in my own little world. A world in which he was still pining over me. He couldn't have started up with someone else so fast. Especially not a girl like her. And he certainly couldn't have been kissing Ivy in front of Pemberly. He was Josh. A gentleman. A thoughtful, caring, sensitive person. He just couldn't.

As I watched, Josh leaned even closer to Ivy and hot anger shot through me. Did he really have to be so public about it? Did he really have to rub my face in whatever he and Ivy had? I was going to find a date who would put Josh to shame. I would do it if it killed me. And I was also going to find some way to prove that Ivy had been stalking me. He could never be with her if he knew that. Right?

My phone trilled, knocking me out of my daze. I fished it out of my bag quickly and checked the screen. The call was coming from the manager of the St. Sebastian.

"It's Cheryl Wallace," I told Noelle.

Her brows knit as I answered it, which gave me a thump of foreboding. Did this mean that something was wrong?

"Hello?" I answered.

"Hello, Miss Brennan. This is Cheryl Wallace from the Saint Sebastian," a woman's voice said pleasantly. "How are you this morning?"

"Fine. How are you?" I asked, confused.

"Well, I have some bad news, unfortunately," she said.

I automatically turned away from my friends, swinging my legs into the aisle between tables. "Bad news?" I repeated, lowering my voice.

"Yes. I'm afraid there was some sort of snafu with our scheduling program," Cheryl said. "It seems your date has been booked for weeks."

"What?" I blurted loudly. "No. That's not possible."

Everyone at the two Billings tables fell silent, as did half the dining hall. I placed my hand on my forehead as my heart began a panicked dance inside my chest.

"I'm so sorry, Miss Brennan, but there's nothing I can do."

"No. There must be something. The fund-raiser is less than a week away," I said desperately, closing my eyes against the curious stares. "We signed a contract. We . . . we put down a deposit."

"Which will be refunded in full, of course," she said politely.

"You're not getting it," I replied, my voice so tense I barely recognized it. "The invitations have already been sent. You can't—"

"Again, Miss Brennan. I'm very sorry. But—"

"Don't tell me there's nothing you can do!" I shouted. "Who booked the place? Maybe I can call them and convince them to—"

"I'm afraid I can't share that information," Cheryl said, clucking her tongue.

"But you have to! There has to be something I can—"

"Please accept my apologies, Miss Brennan. I'll put your check in the mail today."

With that, she hung up and I started to hyperventilate. I placed my phone on the table and slowly turned around, resting my elbows on either side of it. I stared down at the screen, willing it to ring again. Willing Cheryl to call back and tell me it was all a joke. A misunderstanding. But the phone lay still and silent.

"Reed, what is it? What's going on?" Tiffany asked.

"She said . . . she said the place had already been booked. They messed up," I replied, looking up at all of them desperately. "She says there's nothing she can do."

The Billings Girls stared back at me, shocked. I had let them down. I had let them all down.

"There goes the fund-raiser," Missy said finally.

"And Billings," Rose added, looking ill.

Tears stung my eyes. What were we going to do? I had let them all down. Every one of them. I was going to go down in history as the president who killed Billings.

"All right, all right. Everyone calm down," Noelle said loudly. "I happen to have a backup plan."

"You do?" Vienna asked.

"You do?" I echoed, feeling a rush of hope.

Noelle looked at me and folded her arms in front of her on the table. "I booked Loft Blanc," she told me. There was something approaching an apology in her eyes. "Just in case."

"You what?" I blurted, my relief turning to anger. "Why would you—"

"Just in case," she repeated. "When you throw together an event this fast, it's always good to have a backup."

My skin started a slow burn. All day Sunday she had acted as if she had come around to my way of thinking. That the St. Sebastian was the best venue for our event. But all the while, she had already gone behind my back and booked the place she had wanted. She had been hoping something like this would happen. I could see it in her eyes.

"Noelle! You are a genius!" London cried, getting up and hugging Noelle from behind.

"What would we do without you?" Vienna added.

Suddenly everyone was getting up, congratulating Noelle. A few people even golf clapped for her achievement. And I had to sit there and watch it all. Watch them thank her for saving my ass. Watch her preen at the attention.

No matter what I did, no matter how hard I worked, it was always Noelle who saved the day. Always Noelle who got the credit.

DIABOLICAL

"I am so glad Noelle had a backup plan," Constance gushed as she slid into the seat next to mine in calc class that afternoon. "I swear, when you said that place had been booked already, I saw my life flash before my eyes. I mean, to get into Billings and then have it shut down? That would be so not fair."

"Yeah. Thank God for Noelle," I grumbled halfheartedly, taking out my heavy calculus tome.

Sabine and Missy looked at each other as they took their own seats nearby, and both scoffed in unison. That was interesting. I was pretty sure I'd never seen those two connect on anything. Ever.

"What?" I asked warily. The rest of the classroom started to fill in around us, but Mr. Crandle hadn't arrived yet.

"You know that Noelle booked the St. Sebastian herself," Sabine said, perching on the edge of her chair. "Who else has the money to pay for the venue *and* bribe them to lie to you?"

My heart tumbled down along my rib cage. "What are you talking about? What do you mean, lie?"

Missy laughed and shook her head as she opened her notebook. It was all I could do to keep from elbowing her in the face.

"We were there, Reed. We all saw their schedule. There was nothing booked for this Saturday," Sabine said in a soothing tone, like she was explaining a deathly diagnosis to a delicate cancer patient. "The only way this could have happened would be if some-one called up *after* we booked it and offered them more money."

"No," I said, shaking my head, even as my cheeks turned pink with irritation. "She wouldn't do that."

I might have been irritated that Noelle always seemed to manage to save the day, but I couldn't believe she'd actually plot against me. That she would set up a situation just so that she would *have* to swoop in and fix things.

"Yeah. No way," Constance agreed.

"Oh, please. Would you wake up already?" Missy said incredulously. "Did you not go to school here last year? What would Noelle *not* do to get her way?"

"Nothing," Sabine agreed. "She couldn't handle the fact that you made all the decisions this weekend, so she set up a problem so that she could fix it. Now she looks like the hero."

"It's perfect, really," Missy added as Mr. Crandle entered the room, dropping his leather briefcase on his desk. "Diabolical, but perfect."

"No. I can't believe she would orchestrate something like this," I said. "I just—"

"You're clouded by your friendship," Sabine whispered, leaning toward me. "But I can see her for what she really is, and trust me, that girl doesn't care about anyone but herself."

Before I could respond, she turned and resolutely faced the front of the room, unwilling to hear more. I glanced at Constance, who simply shrugged.

"Everyone kindly open your books to page one hundred fifteen," Mr. Crandle announced as he started writing an equation on the board. "I hope you're all ready to concentrate, because this is going to be an intense day."

Tell me about it.

I sighed and opened my book, trying to put thoughts of Noelle and the fund-raiser out of my mind, but I couldn't. I couldn't stop thinking about Sabine's last words. That Noelle didn't care about anyone but herself.

I was starting to think she might be right.

After classes I walked slowly across the quad, taking my time on my way back to Billings. I thought about stopping for coffee, but didn't want to feel more jittery than I already did. I thought about going to the library, but I knew I wouldn't be able to concentrate on studying. Besides, I was supposed to be helping my friends with the fund-raiser. There was no avoiding it. I had to go home.

But maybe I would just stop for my mail first. And read it all in front of my P.O. box. Even the catalogs. Anything to avoid Billings. Avoid the merriment. And, of course, my room.

Even though there was a murder investigation going on, Billings had suddenly become the most animated space south of the North Pole. My friends, it seemed, had chosen to ignore the morbid and throw themselves into the fund-raiser. To deal with the problem they could actually solve. I should have been happy to see them rushing home to put together gift bags and make place cards and schedule makeover appointments. I should have felt gratified that everyone was behind my plan. But I wasn't. I was depressed.

It no longer felt like my plan—it felt like Noelle's. It no longer felt like my night, considering I couldn't even bring the guy I wanted to bring. At least I knew that Ivy and Josh wouldn't be attending the event. No one was more anti-Billings than those two, so I couldn't imagine either one of them putting up the funds for admission. Luckily, I wouldn't have to watch them canoodling all night. Of course, that also meant they'd be back here at Easton, with practically the whole campus to themselves. They could canoodle all over the place if they wanted to.

Great. Now I was even more depressed.

Part of me was actually looking forward to going home for Thanksgiving next week. Go figure.

I shoved open the post office door and walked over to my mailbox, quickly working the lock. Inside there was only one envelope—large, red, and square—with my name and address printed in gold. Intrigued, I tore right into it. The lining of the envelope was purple, and the invitation inside was round and black.

An invitation to Kiran Hayes's eighteenth birthday party.

My heart leapt as if I'd just been accepted to Harvard. Kiran remembered me. She had actually included me in her plans.

I went to shove the invite back in the envelope and noticed a piece of heavy white card stock nestled inside. The initials *K. H.* were stamped at the top. Underneath was a handwritten note from Kiran.

> *Reed,*
> *It's been TOO long. Please come. Would love to catch up.*
> *x's,*
> *Kiran*

Okay. So maybe things were finally starting to look up. Grinning from ear to ear, I walked back to the doors. Standing at the counter near the exit was Marc, picking up a rather large package. His face lit up when he saw me. Which was nice.

"Hey!" he said, sliding the box off the counter and wrapping both arms around it in front of him. His fingers barely made it around the sides. "What's up?"

"Nothing. Just picked up my mail," I replied. "That's a big box."

"My grandmother. She thinks I'm going to freeze to death up here, so every winter she sends me a whole mess of homemade sweaters. She even took a knitting class so she could make them look more professional, since I go to school with all those, quote, 'fashion plates.'"

God, he was so normal. And sweet, actually appreciating his grandmother and all. If I couldn't go to the fund-raiser with Josh, this was the person I wanted to go with. Someone who wouldn't spend all night seeking my attention or looking down my dress or getting drunk off his ass and being an embarrassment. And so I just said it.

"Marc, do you want to be my date for the fund-raiser?" I asked.

His eyebrows shot up and he readjusted the box, tossing it up to get a better grip near the bottom. "Seriously?"

"Seriously."

"I'd be honored," he replied with a grin. "Escorting the woman of the hour. It would be my extreme pleasure."

I laughed. It was nice to hear that someone I actually respected thought of me that way. "Thanks. I'll, um . . . I'll give you all the info tomorrow."

I would have e-mailed it to him, but I had that whole computer-avoidance issue.

"Sounds good," Marc replied, starting past me, awkwardly managing the box and his hefty backpack, which had slid down and now hung from his elbow. "Thanks for asking me."

"Thanks for saying yes," I replied with a smile.

As Marc hobbled out, I felt about ten times better. I was invited to Kiran's party, and I had a date for the fund-raiser, with someone I might actually want to talk to, at that. I knew the Billings Girls wouldn't approve—they would have preferred a Hunter Braden, even if he was a jackass—but at that moment I didn't care. Maybe it was time for this Billings president to start doing things her own way.

SAFE

When I walked into Billings, Noelle was standing near the fireplace in the foyer with Tiffany and the Twin Cities while Sabine, Constance, Kiki, and Astrid pored over a printout of the guest list. Noelle turned and her eyes went right to the invitation, which was still clutched in my hand.

"Oh, good. You got one. I thought I was going to have to text Kiran and remind her to invite you," she said.

All the blood in my body rushed right to my head and started to boil. Like I needed her help to land an invite. Like I would be nowhere without her.

"So, Reed," Noelle continued, as if she hadn't just insulted me, "since the whole night is about glamour, we were talking about maybe hiring some models to just circulate around the room and look hot. What do you think of—"

Without a word, I turned and stormed up the stairs, taking them two at a time. I could practically feel the hushed surprise at my rudeness following me all the way up to my room, but I didn't care. I was so sick of Noelle. So sick of her constantly trying to put me in my place. As if she could define what my place was. Maybe last year. Maybe last year I had let her do that. But not anymore.

The door opened behind me and I whirled around, expecting to find Noelle walking in without a knock as always. But it was Sabine. A very timid-looking Sabine.

"What was that?" she half-whispered. "Are you okay?"

"Actually, no. I'm not," I blurted, throwing my coat down on my bed. "I'm starting to think you're right about Noelle. I mean, I always just figured that her little digs and stuff were just part of her personality, and I let them roll off my back or whatever, but now I'm starting to wonder why I need to be friends with a person who treats people like that. When does it stop? When do we become good enough friends that she stops wanting to make me feel like shit?"

I had no idea there was so much venom inside of me until it started spewing out. I took a deep breath and looked at the floor.

"Maybe you're right. Maybe the only person she cares about is herself."

"Well, have you ever seen her be consistently nice to any of her friends?" Sabine asked.

I thought back to last year. Back to her random jabs at Taylor and that whole incident with Kiran and her Dreck boy. She certainly hadn't treated either of those so-called BFFs with much respect. But then there was the other.

"Ariana," I said bitterly. "She's the only one Noelle never put down."

Sabine stared at me. I knew the name didn't hold as much power with her as it did with me, but she had heard the story. She knew enough to know that Ariana was an interesting choice when it came to showing loyalty.

"If one of your friends has you paranoid . . . constantly walking around wondering when she's going to choose to backstab you . . . then that person isn't much of a friend," Sabine said finally, biting her lip.

And she had a very good point. Last year I had needed Noelle and the other Billings Girls. Their friendship had seemed so important to me—to helping me leave my old life behind and become the person I wanted to be here at Easton. But now I *was* that person. I was Billings president. And all those other girls were gone. Everyone but Noelle. Did I really need her hanging around, constantly reminding me of how lucky I was to know her?

Definitely not.

The door opened.

"Reed, we have to talk," Noelle said.

I looked at her. Looked at Sabine. My chest was heaving from all my running and ranting. My heart pounded in my ears. What to say? How to handle this?

"Do you mind?" Noelle said to Sabine.

"She can stay," I snapped. "This *is* her room, not yours. This house is not yours. I may have thought it was once, but I was wrong. It doesn't all belong to you. We don't all belong to you."

Noelle took a deep breath. She crossed her arms over her chest and looked at me "Okay. So obviously you're pissed off about something."

My skin tingled as I faced off with her. I felt like I was about to go into battle. Like I was Russell Crowe in that gladiator movie my brother was so obsessed with, standing just outside the gates of the Colosseum, listening to the crowd that was salivating for my blood.

"Try a lot of things," I replied.

"You still think I'm trying to take over," Noelle theorized. Sabine quietly moved away and sat down on the edge of her desk chair from the side, watching us.

"You're not?"

Noelle rolled her eyes and tipped her head back. "Reed, we both have the same goal here. We're both just trying to save Billings. God, this is more for you than me. You're still going to be here next year. Do you *want* to spend your senior year in Pemberly?"

"That's not what this is about. This is about you trying to sabotage me," I replied, crossing my arms as well.

"Sabotage you?" Noelle's face screwed up in confusion. "What are you smoking?"

"Did you or did you not call back Cheryl after we left and convince her to say the place was booked?" I demanded, my face hot at my own audacity.

Noelle appeared shocked. But was she? "What?"

"I think you did. I think you knew all along that the St. Sebastian was going to fall through and that's why you booked Loft Blanc," I told her. "It's vintage Noelle. Not only do you get your way, but you get to swoop in and look like the hero to everyone in the process."

"You're cracked!" Noelle said sharply. "I would never do something like that."

"Oh, wouldn't you?" I shot back.

Noelle took a deep breath and pushed her hands through her hair, lifting it back from her face. "Okay. Don't get me wrong. There's a lot I'd do to get my way, but do you have any idea what a huge waste that would have been? My family may have a lot of money, Reed, but we didn't get where we are by burning huge piles of it for no apparent reason."

"Yeah. Right."

"Look, I only booked Loft Blanc because I've been through this before," Noelle told me, lifting a hand. "Two summers ago, my cousin's wedding got canceled the week before the ceremony because the place she booked went under. It was a total nightmare. Ever since then my mother has booked two venues for every important party we've hosted. And I think you know that this is one hell of an important party."

I stared at Noelle's face. For once her expression was completely without guile. She looked almost desperate. Desperate for me to believe her. And, to be honest, I'd never heard her try to explain herself so vehemently in my life.

"Swear you didn't book the St. Sebastian," I demanded.

Sabine shifted in her seat, and I knew she was annoyed that I was caving, but I ignored her.

"Reed, I swear," Noelle said.

I tipped my head forward and covered my face with my hands. Crap. I believed her. I so wanted to be all indignant and right, but I believed her.

"So are we okay?" Noelle asked.

"No," I blurted. "No. We're not."

Her brow creased as I looked up at her again. "Why not?"

"You have to stop, Noelle," I said, rounding my shoulders. "You have to stop treating me like I'm some moronic little peon to be mocked. I'm not Glass-Licker anymore. I'm the president of this house. And I'm supposed to be your friend. You have to stop . . . picking on me. As lame as that sounds."

I expected her to smirk. To say something condescending about how cute I was or something. But she merely looked stricken.

"I'm not going to take it anymore," I told her. "We're either friends . . . equals . . . or we're not. So which is it gonna be?"

Noelle blew out a sigh. She walked past me and sat on the edge of my bed. She looked so confused and displaced. Like she was going through an out-of-body experience. Which maybe she was. There was a good chance no one had ever called her on her behavior before.

"Noelle?" I prompted.

"We're friends," she said, looking up at me, her eyes huge. "Equals."

"You're sure about that."

"Reed, you and I . . . we've been through so much together. Thomas and Ariana and all that crap around the Legacy last year and this thing with Dash . . . "

I glanced over at Sabine, who looked at me curiously. Yeah. That was the first time she'd ever heard about any "thing with Dash."

"Honestly? I would have annihilated anyone else who pulled what you pulled, but I forgave you without a blink. Think about that," Noelle said firmly. "How could you ever doubt that we're friends?"

My heart expanded so quickly I thought it might fill up my chest and crack my ribs. I had never heard Noelle sound so sincere. So vulnerable. I was starting to regret having let Sabine stay. I knew that in the light of day, Noelle was going to hate the fact that anyone other than me had seen her like this.

"So . . . why do you treat me the way you do? What's with all the backhanded comments and put-downs?" I asked.

Noelle stood up again and hugged herself, as if she'd just gotten a chill. "I don't know. Maybe it's because you're kind of like the little sister I never had. You're supposed to mess with your little sister, right?" she joked halfheartedly.

"True," I said, thinking of Scott. "Or in the case of my family, torture them, steal their tooth fairy money, and blame them for everything."

Noelle chuckled. "I really have to meet your brother sometime."

Now that would be interesting.

She took a deep breath. "But anyway, I'll stop if you want me to stop. Or at least I'll try. I can't guarantee a total personality over-haul."

"Thanks."

We both stood there for a moment awkwardly, not knowing what to do. I felt deflated. Exhausted. All that adrenaline and anger had been sucked right out of me so fast I was almost light-headed.

"So, should we hug or something?" Noelle suggested finally.

"Sure."

So we did. And for the first time in a long time, I felt safe. I still had Noelle on my side. I hadn't realized how uncertain the threat of breaking free of her had made me feel. If there was anyone at Easton I needed, it was her. The girl who had taken me under her wing. The girl who had saved my life. The girl who had convinced me to come back after I'd decided to drop out. I could never let myself forget that again.

BECAUSE OF ME

The rest of the week passed in a whirlwind of phone calls from florists and caterers and drivers and alumni. There was some insanity when we discovered that London and Vienna had taken it upon themselves to run with the models-as-moving-art idea and had each hired twenty guys—and no girls—by luring them into working for free with the promise of the amazing contacts they could make. Luckily we managed to fix the problem in time and hire twenty girls. Somehow in there I managed to write a paper for Spanish and ace a history test. Apparently, I was a good multitasker.

The best part of the whole week was that the stalking had stopped. Maybe Ivy had gotten bored or busy or scared after her trip to the police station, but whatever the reason, the whole week passed without another incident. On Wednesday, I went to the administration office and changed my e-mail address for the second time, promising myself that I would give this one only to teachers and family. My friends could text my phone if they wanted to—I didn't care. All that mattered to me was never seeing Cheyenne's name in my in-box again.

As for Dash's e-mail, it was just going to have to go unread. And so what? He was Noelle's boyfriend now. If she was going to try to change for me, the least I could do was quit her man cold turkey.

By the time Saturday morning rolled around and we were all piling our luggage and makeup cases and garment bags outside the front door of Billings for our chauffeurs to take to the cars, I was feeling pretty damn good about myself and about the house. I gathered everyone into the foyer, climbed to the third step of the staircase, and shouted for everyone's attention. They fell silent instantly. Fifteen pairs of interested eyes looked up at me, riveted. This was power.

"I just wanted to thank everyone for all your hard work these past couple of weeks," I announced, gripping the banister. I lifted my blue folder, which contained the guest list and all the spreadsheets breaking down received donations and pledged donations. "And although my father always says, 'Never count a chicken before it's hatched,' I think it's safe to say that with all the money we've already made, and all the money we stand to make at Tassos's silent auction tonight, we will more than reach our goal."

Everyone cheered and hugged and congratulated one another. I watched it all from my perch, feeling like I'd really done it. I'd saved our home. This was all because of me.

As I watched my friends giddily trail out the door to head for our waiting limousines, I even had a stray thought of Cheyenne and how proud she would be. I felt warmed by the idea.

"Reed! Reed!" Rose jogged back inside with a vase full of white roses. "These were just delivered for you!"

Vienna, London, Rose, and Noelle all gathered around while I read the card.

"They're from Marc," I said happily. "He says good luck and he'll see me tonight."

"I think we underestimated Scholarship Boy," London said, earning a pointed glare from Noelle. Was it a good thing or a bad thing that my friends kept forgetting that I was on scholarship?

"White roses. A smart choice," Vienna mused. "Red would be too pushy, pink would be too babyish, but white . . . white is . . ."

"Elegant. Refined," Noelle said, taking the vase from my hands and placing it in the center of the mantel. "The kid's good."

I smiled, glad they were coming around. Even if I didn't intend to seriously date the guy, it was nice to know my friends had some depth.

"We should get out of here. We have to beat the traffic," I said, hustling the stragglers out.

Everyone rushed ahead into the cold as I paused to close the door behind us. The two chauffeurs were just gathering up the last of our things and I was about to thank them when I saw something move out of the corner of my eye. Ivy . Speed-walking away from Billings toward Pemberly. My heart stopped at the sight of her. What had she been doing over here? And why was she in such a rush? She was moving so quickly and was so oblivious to her surroundings that she practically mowed over Amberly Carmichael and her group of followers, who had paused for a chat on one of the paths.

"See you tonight, Reed! We can't wait!" Amberly called out to me, waving a mittened hand.

I took a deep breath and told myself to forget about Ivy. Right now I had to get through tonight and declare a Billings victory. Then I could deal with her.

"See you there!" I shouted back.

I jogged across the quad to catch up with my friends, past Bradwell to the circle, where the limos idled near the curb. Everyone randomly piled into the cars, intent on getting out of the cold. As I settled in and looked around, I found that I had ended up with most of the seniors. Noelle, Tiffany, London, Vienna, Rose, Portia, and Shelby. Tiffany reached into a vat of ice built into the door and extracted a bottle of champagne.

"Let's get this celebration started!" she announced, popping it open.

Everyone cheered as foam washed over the side of the bottle onto the floor. We squealed and pulled our feet back, out of the line of fire. As the car pulled away from the curb, Rose passed around champagne flutes and Tiffany clumsily poured.

"I would like to propose a toast!" Noelle announced, lifting her glass once everyone had been served. "To Reed!"

"To Reed!" everyone chorused, lifting their glasses.

"No, ladies. I wasn't finished," Noelle admonished with a sly look.

Champagne sloshed everywhere as the limo hit the speed bump near the bottom of the hill, and we all laughed.

"This girl has saved Billings, she's landed herself an *adorable* boy and has half a dozen more pursuing her, and she looks simply fabulous," Noelle continued.

I blushed and my friends cracked up laughing.

"What I'm trying to say is, you clearly chose wisely when you chose our president," Noelle said, looking me in the eye. Everyone murmured their agreement. My heart was about to burst. "To Reed."

"To Reed!"

It was one of the best moments of my life.

BEST FRIENDS

I loved that I was sipping champagne in a salon on Park Avenue with a sign on the door that read CLOSED FOR PRIVATE EVENT. I loved that people kept stopping on the street and peeking in, trying to get a glimpse of what fabulousness might be occurring inside. I loved the way it felt to be on the inside looking out, instead of the outside looking in.

It was one of those moments when I realized absolutely and unequivocally how lucky I was. How the hell did I, Reed Brennan from Croton, Pennsylvania, end up here, talking to a U.S. senator about which eye shadow she should go with while Frederica Falk lined the lips of a famous morning news anchor, and twin fashion heiresses swapped nightmare customs stories with my friends over in the corner?

Unreal.

"So. This is going well," Noelle said, sidling up to me as the senator politely took her leave. But not before pressing a check into my hand.

I unfolded the check and my eyes widened at the number. I held it up for Noelle to see. "I'll say."

She smiled. "That's nothing. Check out the wad that Tweedle Dum and Tweedle Dumber over there handed to Tiffany so they could have a closed set during their shoot with Tassos."

She turned around, her back to the crowd, and pulled out a rolled-up stack of bills that was so thick it could have been used as a paperweight.

I laughed and swigged my champagne. "I hate to be vulgar, but Cromwell is going to shit."

"Can I be there when it happens?" Noelle asked, tucking the money away again.

"Absolutely."

We both smiled, enjoying the warmth of the moment. This was going to work out. The fund-raiser, our friendship, everything. It was all going to work out.

"There! Perfection!" Frederica announced as she finished with the anchorwoman. All afternoon this had been her signal that she was done with a client, and the entire room fell silent at the sound of her pinched, heavily accented voice. Frederica was a diminutive German woman with platinum blond hair and tiny horn-rimmed glasses, who—even though she couldn't have been taller than five feet—had a commanding presence. When she spoke, people listened.

"And now, for the organizer of our event," Frederica said. She marched over to me, all bones and black turtleneck and slicked-back hair, and grabbed my shoulders. "I must do you!"

"What? Me? No," I protested. "This event is for our donors—"

"Nonsense! None of them would be here if not for you!" she said, forcibly turning me toward her chair. "And I must work on this flawless face," she added, tapping my cheeks with her cold hands from behind as we looked in the mirror. "You cannot say no."

"She's right, Reed," Noelle said, taking my champagne glass from me. "It's a once-in-a-lifetime type of thing to have Frederica work her magic."

My friends and their guests and all the alumni in the salon were either eyeing me enviously for being singled out, or encouraging me to seize the opportunity.

"Sit," Fredericka ordered, forcibly pushing me into the chair. She was stronger than her scrawny body let on. "We do this now."

"All right, then," I said, looking in the mirror at the waiting clientele, the women getting their blowouts and the others in black smocks, still waiting their turns. "If no one else minds."

No one said a word. Apparently, in a room full of luminaries and debutantes and zillionaires, I was the one person allowed to cut the line.

"I'll go refill your champagne," Noelle said, squeezing my shoulder before disappearing into the crowd.

I smiled and settled back in the chair. All day Noelle had been by my side and not once had she hit me with a derisive comment or a sneer or even a slightly condescending look. And now she was running off to get me champagne like it was no big deal. Like she didn't covet the position I was in. Like she didn't mind doing things for me at all.

Maybe we really were best friends.

I had been inside a few Manhattan dwellings in the past two years. The first two—Thomas Pearson's apartment and the Legacy locale from last October—I didn't remember much about. I had been dizzy with grief and confusion when I'd visited the Pearson home, and it wasn't as if his parents had given everyone the grand tour during their son's wake. All I recalled was that it seemed large and cold and overly furnished. The Legacy penthouse was even more of a blur, considering how drunk I'd gotten and how dark it had been. I remembered thinking it was huge, and that the view of Central Park was amazing. The third, Josh Hollis's downtown brownstone, was nice. Cozy. Tricked out with all the modern amenities, but with a feeling like a real family home. And I didn't want to think about it any further than that.

Noelle's house, however, was astonishing. It was like a full-blown mansion nestled in the middle of an otherwise unassuming block.

From the outside it looked like a posh apartment building with its grand staircase and big, red door complete with a gold knocker. It looked large enough to be divided into eight or ten units. But it wasn't. It was one unit. One, huge, gorgeous, pristine, divine unit.

Sabine and I must have looked like awed tourists at Versailles as Noelle led us through the foyer toward the back of the house and the elevator. We all shed our coats as we went, and handed them to one of three waiting maids, who followed after us silently. I almost tripped peeking into the rooms that lined the long entryway—a library with more books than the Croton library could ever hope to own, a conservatory with a grand piano, a sitting room like something out of an Austen novel. This place was sick.

But no one else seemed to notice. Not even Constance. Which made me wonder what their houses were like.

Noelle's room, where we would all be staying that night, was situated on the fourth of five floors. In fact, her room *was* the fourth floor. It was more of a suite, with an enormous bedroom, a sitting room with a TV the size of a movie screen, a walk-in closet with rows and rows of clothes, and a pink-marble bathroom I could have gotten lost in. It also had a mini kitchen stocked with snacks and a state-of-the art espresso machine, and its own outdoor patio overlooking the park. My whole family could have lived in Noelle's suite comfortably.

"All right, make yourselves pretty!" Noelle announced, tossing her bag and dress on her four-poster bed. "Use whatever you need. Except the stuff in my special cosmetics cabinet. Oh, but I had a lock put on that anyway. Since I don't trust any of you," she joked.

Everyone laughed and went about unpacking their things. We didn't have much time before the start of the dinner and silent auction, so we dressed quickly, all sixteen of us in the same room—zipping each other's dresses, clasping necklaces, buckling straps on shoes. As soon as everyone was clothed, there was a race for the bathroom and dressing rooms with their well-lit mirrors. I stayed behind with Noelle. My makeup had already been done by a professional.

"Noelle, this place is amazing," I said, walking over to the glass sliders that led to the patio. The short hem of my gold dress skimmed my thighs and the smooth fabric made me feel decadent. "Not what I would have imagined, though."

"No?" she asked, fastening a sparking sapphire necklace around her neck as she joined me. "Why not?"

"Because it's not a huge mess," I replied with a smirk.

She smiled in return. "I have my own staff, Reed. Believe me, this place did not look like this when last I left."

She turned to an oak cabinet and slid open the doors. "Music?"

Inside was a sleek stereo system surrounded by shelves and shelves of CDs and old-school records. An iPod was hooked up to the system, but there was also a CD player and a record player standing by.

"Wow. I had no idea you were so into music," I said, running my fingers along the spines of the albums. A lot of my dad's favorite classics were represented. Everything from the Beatles to the Doors to the Clash to U2 and hundreds of bands in between.

"It's my obsession," Noelle said, shrugging. She selected a CD and popped it in. "Concerts are my anti-drug," she said with a wry smile.

As music poured through speakers in every corner and Noelle disappeared into her closet for shoes, I realized there was a lot I didn't know about her. Did she like to read? If so, what? What did she like to watch on that huge TV screen of hers? And I knew she liked to travel, but where? What did she and Dash do together for fun? Maybe we weren't as good friends as I had started to believe we were. But I could remedy that. Starting now.

I reached into my bag for my new perfume and popped off the cap. "So, what was the last concert you saw?" I shouted to be heard in the depths of her closet.

I spritzed the perfume just as Portia, Rose, Tiffany, and Sabine returned from the bathroom, gabbing away. The scent filled my senses and I instantly gagged.

Cheyenne. It smelled like Cheyenne. The scent was in my nose, on my clothes, in my hair, floating in the air all around me. Cheyenne's scent. Cheyenne's signature sweet, flowery scent. The other girls froze in their tracks.

"Did you just spray Fleur?" Rose asked, confused.

"That's a little weird, Reed. Cheyenne's perfume?" Portia said.

"No! I—"

I glanced down at the bottle. It was a small round atomizer with the word FLEUR printed across it in smoky white letters. Where had this come from? I hadn't packed this. I checked the bag I'd extracted it from to make sure it was mine, and it was. My pajamas, my book, my makeup bag.

"I didn't bring this," I said, feeling dizzy. The scent was in my head now. Making me foggy even as my heartbeat pounded against my chest. "I packed the bottle I bought at Barneys last weekend. I swear. It was called Free, remember?" I said, looking to Sabine for confirmation.

"Well, maybe you picked up this one instead when you were packing," Sabine replied, looking a little concerned.

"No. I don't own any other perfume," I snapped, feeling like a caged dog. "That was the first bottle I've ever bought."

Noelle emerged from the closet at that moment and saw everyone staring at me. "Reed? What's wrong?"

I took a couple shaky steps back and dropped onto the edge of her bed. "This isn't mine. I didn't bring this. I didn't buy it. I would never . . . I'd never want to smell like . . . Somebody must have put it in my bag."

I looked up at all of them, wide-eyed, my pulse visible in my wrists, and they simply stared back, disturbed. Disturbed and confused and worried.

"Reed, why would anyone put Cheyenne's perfume in your bag?" Tiffany asked.

"I don't know!" I wailed, shaking and on the verge of tears. Her scent was all over me. Choking me. "Why would anyone do any of the things they're doing? Why would anyone—"

I stopped abruptly, realizing I'd said too much. A few of the other girls had joined us now and everyone was watching me as if I were an escaped lunatic.

"What things?" Rose asked, hugging herself.

I glanced around the room. I couldn't tell them. They were going to think I was insane. And maybe I was. Maybe I was losing my mind.

"I have to get out of this dress," I said, standing and grabbing for the zipper behind my neck. My hands were so slippery with sweat they couldn't grasp the zipper. "Get me out of it. Somebody unzip it!" I demanded.

Constance rushed forward and undid the zip. Cool air rushed all over my skin and I let it fall to the floor, kicking it aside. "I can't wear that. It smells like her," I rambled, standing in front of all of them in my one and only set of lacy underwear. Goose bumps covered my bare skin, and I was starting to lose my breath. "I can't wear that. I have to wear something else."

"Reed, calm down." Noelle broke through my line of horrified onlookers and grasped my arm. "You can wear something of mine. It's all good."

"Are you okay?" Sabine asked, as Noelle led me back through the crowd toward her closet. "Do you need anything?"

"Just get rid of that bottle. I don't care what you do with it," I said, gasping for air. I glanced at the offending bottle that I'd left on Noelle's bedspread. "Just get rid of it."

As soon as we were inside the closet, Noelle closed the door and sat me down on a suede bench between racks of clothes. Tears stung my eyes and spilled down my cheeks. I braced my hands on the bench at my sides and squirmed, gasping for air. The photo and the black marbles and the clothing and the e-mails and now this. It was all too much.

"Reed, you have to breathe," Noelle told me, kneeling in her black dress in front of me. "You're freaking me out here. Please breathe."

I gulped for air, but it stopped at my throat. It wouldn't go through to my lungs.

"Put your head between your legs."

She forced my head down and I saw spots, but the next breath hit home. My lungs burned as I sucked in air and coughed, tears of pain now coursing down my face, dropping onto the thick white carpet at my feet.

"That's it. Breathe," Noelle told me in a soothing voice. "Breathe."

When I finally started to return to normal, I sat up and took in a nice, long breath of air. I wiped my eyes and came away with black streaks. So much for my professional makeover.

"Better?" she asked.

I managed to nod.

"*What* is going on?" She got up from the floor and sat next to me. "What was that all about?"

I wanted to tell her, but I couldn't. I had just earned her respect. I couldn't tell her that someone at Easton was screwing with me. Or that I was quite possibly losing my mind. I couldn't show her just how vulnerable I was. Not now.

Suddenly, now that my head was clear, I remembered. Remembered seeing Ivy just before we left Easton, beating a hasty retreat away from Billings. All our bags had been stacked outside for at least fifteen minutes. She could have done this. She could have switched out my bottle of Free for a bottle of Fleur. After all, she could have easily figured out which bag was mine—my initials were embroidered on it. It had to have been her. It was the only explanation that made any sense.

"Reed?" Noelle prompted.

I looked up at my friend, at her concerned face, but I knew I couldn't tell her. Not yet. Not until I was sure. So I did something I'd found myself doing a lot lately. I lied.

"I don't know. I don't . . . I don't know how that perfume got in my bag, but the second I sprayed it, I guess it just all came rushing back," I replied. "Cheyenne always wore that perfume. I guess it just brought it all back so vividly—finding her body, how awful that day was. . . . I don't know."

Noelle pushed my hair behind my shoulder and ran her hand down the length of it in a comforting way. "Are you sure that's it? There's nothing else you want to tell me?"

"No," I said, sniffling. "I just lost it for a second there. I'm sorry." I stood up and squared my shoulders, trying to show her I was okay. "Are you sure you don't mind me borrowing a dress?" Noelle stood as well and turned toward the section of her closet where little black dresses hung in neat rows. "Take your pick. As long as you're sure you're okay."

"I'm fine," I lied. "I have to be. I have a fund-raiser to run."

Noelle smiled in a proud way. "That's my little—I mean, good for you," she said with a nod, correcting herself. "I'll go tell them you're okay. You just get dressed and clean yourself up." She picked up a

Charles David shoe box and extracted a small gold key from the toe of a stiletto heel inside. "You can even use the special cosmetics."

"Thanks."

I smiled as she slipped out and closed the door behind her. The moment she was gone, I sat down at the dressing table and stared at myself in the mirror. Eyeliner dripped down my face, and the cream blush that had been so carefully applied was all but gone. I looked like a sad clown who'd been caught in a rainstorm. Scary. Freakish. Insane.

How was I going to do this? How was I going to pull this night off while feeling like I was about to lose my mind?

I stared into my puffy eyes and took a deep breath. Outside, the Billings Girls were chatting happily, my frantic moment clearly forgotten.

"You have to do this, Reed. For them. For Billings," I told myself, even as my heartbeat pounded in my ears. "You can get fitted for your straitjacket later."

MINE

Noelle had been right all along. Loft Blanc was the perfect location for this event. It was simple. Minimal. Clean. Glamorous. And with the champagne flowing, the chatter filling the room, and the Twin Cities' model brigade circulating in skimpy clothes with their placid expressions, it was all like one decadent work of moving art.

I saw all this. Processed it. But couldn't appreciate it. All I could think about was the perfume.

The next time I saw Ivy I was going to make her confess. And then I was going to kick her ass. Enough was enough.

"Reed! Congratulations! This event is a smash hit!" Susan Llewelyn said, stopping by to double air-kiss me. Susan was one of the few Billings alumnae I actually knew.

"Thanks," I said, surprised to see her. "Can I ask you something?"

"Of course!" she said, taking a sip of her champagne and tossing her short blond hair back.

"Where were you the day the board met to go over our case?" I asked. "We could have used a friend on the other side."

Susan blinked and her ever-present smile briefly faltered. I got the distinct feeling she thought I had just overstepped my bounds. And maybe I had. But didn't I deserve to know?

"The board felt that my presence would be a conflict of interest," she said smoothly. "And to be honest, I thought it might be a good idea for me to lie low, considering my part in the whole Gwendolyn mess."

"I see."

In other words, she hadn't wanted to be forced to take responsibility for telling us how to get off campus—for leading us to the Gwendolyn secret passageway in the first place. Suddenly, the level of respect I'd always felt for Suzel dropped a notch.

"Oh! I see an old friend! Gotta go!" she said gaily.

As she hastily scurried off, I wondered if anyone was ever what they seemed. So far, most of the people I had met at Easton had turned out to have at least two faces. Some many more.

"Champagne?" Marc asked, suddenly arriving at my side.

He pressed the cool flute against my bare shoulder and I smiled. For a November night, it was rather warm in here, and I was happy I had chosen something skimpy from Noelle's collection. It was a black, halter-style swing dress with subtle pleats that fell a few inches above the knee.

"Thanks," I said, smiling as I took the champagne flute from him.

"Have I told you how amazing you look tonight?" Marc asked.

He looked pretty amazing himself in his rented tux with its long, cocoa brown tie.

"You don't have to say that," I told him, downing half the champagne in one gulp.

"I know I don't. I wanted to," Marc said with a genuine smile.

"Reed. There you are! We've been looking all over for you," Hunter Braden said, appearing before me. He reached out and squeezed my elbow as if he hadn't been the rudest date in history and I hadn't walked out on him. Hunter had gone with a tux and an open-collared shirt, and blond scruff lined his cheeks and chin. Very rogue millionaire. "My mother was dying to meet you. Harper Braden, this is Reed Brennan. She organized this event."

"Mrs. Braden," I said, trying to be warm even though her son basically sucked. "Always a pleasure to meet a Billings alum."

Her blue eyes widened, though I wasn't sure how that was possible, considering she looked as if she had just been shot up with ten vials of Botox in the past hour. Her face was a puffy mask, stretched to its limits around full lips and heavily lined eyes.

"You know your ancient history!" she exclaimed. "Glad to hear it. It's so good to finally meet you." She shook my hand, unsnapped her vintage clutch purse, and extracted a small envelope, which she discreetly handed to me. "For the cause," she said

"Thank you," I replied. Luckily, Cromwell had only said we couldn't accept money from Billings alums for preparations, not for the fund-raising itself.

"Good luck tonight. Not that you'll need it," she added; then she looked past me. "Oh! Is that Rinnan Hearst? I *must* go say hello!"

The mention of the familiar name caused my heart to stop.

I whipped around and there was the famous actress Rinnan Hearst, Cheyenne's stepmother, standing near the wall holding court with Cheyenne's father. One look at his handsome face, his sad eyes, the mournful lines permanently etched around them, and the room started to spin.

"Wow. You really are the woman of the evening," Marc said as a few more people stopped by to congratulate me. People to whom I couldn't even respond. The heavy perfume and sweaty palms assaulted me, and my body temperature skyrocketed. Cheyenne's dad was here. Cheyenne's devastated father. One of the two people who had insisted on reopening her case. Memories assaulted me from every angle. Memories of the way he had barely been able to speak to us on the day of her funeral. Of how he'd fallen to his knees when they released her ashes. He had loved her so much. I could only imagine what it must be like for him, standing in a room full of his daughter's friends, knowing that by all rights she should be there too, chatting and laughing and flirting. Was he wondering who among us might have murdered his daughter? Who might have taken his one and only child from him?

"I have to get out of here," I heard myself say. "I need some air."

"Reed—"

I took one step toward the door and froze. Josh had just walked in. Josh. My savior. My rock. Looking gorgeous in his tux with his curls all askew. Just the sight of him made my heart leap. Why was he here? He hated Billings. Had he come for me? To support me?

Marc was saying something. Had his hand on my wrist as if to calm me. But I couldn't even hear him or feel him or see him. All I saw was Josh. What I wouldn't give to have him back. To feel him hold me. To hear him tell me everything was going to be okay. I felt the longing in my gut, my heart, my skin. So acute it was painful. Suddenly I knew that was what I needed. Not to find someone else to replace him. Not to pick out the perfect specimen to make him jealous. That had all been so petty. So stupid. So vindictive. No. More than anything, I needed him. Josh was all that mattered. He would make it all right.

All I wanted was to hear his voice.

"Josh!" I shouted, not caring that half the room could hear me. "Josh!"

He smiled, but not at me. Smiled at someone coming toward him from his left. The crowd shifted and I saw her. Ivy Slade. Dressed in pure, ironic white. Smiling as Josh took her hand. And the walls crashed in around me.

"What is she doing here?" I snapped venomously.

"Who?" Marc was thoroughly confused at this point.

"After everything she's done . . ."

I was shaking from head to foot from unadulterated anger. How dare she come here tonight? How *dare* she?

"Reed? Who are you talking about?" He followed my gaze and must have spotted Ivy. "Oh. Yeah. That's not good," he said, knowing Ivy was the leader of the anti-Billings brigade.

"She. Cannot. Be here." I started forward, my eyes trained on Ivy. I was going to throw her out. I didn't care if she'd paid to get in. She was the enemy.

"If I can have your attention, please?" Tiffany said into the micro-phone on our small, makeshift stage.

People started to quiet, to turn. I stayed my course. I was on a mission.

"My name is Tiffany Goulbourne, and I'd just like to start out by thanking everyone for coming out tonight."

I was ten steps away. Ten steps away from vindication. From revenge. And then, Josh pulled Ivy to him—pulled her whole body into his—ran his hand over her cheek, and leaned in to kiss her like there was no one else in the room.

I stopped moving. Stopped breathing. Stopped being.

Her eyes fluttered closed. He deepened the kiss, his finger-tips now resting lightly on her shoulder. So it was true. They were together. I had been so hoping it was all a lie. Some out-of-control rumor with a life of its own. So much for hope.

My heart took over. Took over my whole body. Pounding and slam-ming and panicking. Those were my hands. My lips. My fingertips. My tongue. My body. He was mine. Mine, mine, mine.

And yet there he was right in front of me, giving himself to her.

"And now I'd like to bring up the person who is responsible for this fabulous event!" Tiffany's voice boomed through the speakers. "Ladies and gentlemen, Reed Brennan!"

AND THE WINNER IS

I couldn't move. Could not make my limbs bend. Josh and Ivy pulled apart and looked into each other's eyes, their mutual affection blatant, and all I could do was watch.

My head swam. The floor heaved beneath my feet. I was going to faint. Actually going to faint.

"Reed? Where are you, Reed? I know you're out there somewhere!" Tiffany chided, earning polite laughter from the crowd.

Marc stepped up behind me and nudged my arm. "Reed, you have to go. They're waiting for you."

Then Ivy turned and looked up at the stage. She whispered something to Josh and was off, weaving her way with determination through the maze of waiters and guests and models. Where was she going? But wait, who cared? Josh was alone now. All that mattered was—

"Reed! Let's go!"

Suddenly the Twin Cities had me by either arm and were walking me toward Tiffany. The moment I moved, my knees gave out and they had to hold me up for a few steps. The people right around us stared, probably thinking I was drunk. But all I could think about was Josh and Ivy. Josh and Ivy. Josh and Ivy.

How could he kiss her? How could he look at her like that? And at my event. He was supposed to love me. How could he ever look at anyone else that way? It wasn't fair. Didn't he know how evil she was? What she was capable of? He couldn't have known. Would never be with her if he did. I had to tell him the truth about her. I had to tell him that I needed him. I needed—

"Hello, everyone! My name is Ivy Slade and I'm here to tell you all, well, why *you're* really here."

The Twin Cities stopped abruptly and we all gaped up at the stage. Somehow Ivy had gotten the microphone away from Tiffany and was now addressing the rapt crowd.

"This is not a fund-raiser for Easton Academy," Ivy said quickly, vehemently. "It's a PR job for Billings House. You remember Billings House. That tall dorm on the edge of campus where lived the most awful girls at the academy?"

There were a few chuckles. The rest of the Billings Girls, who were dotted throughout the room, started to mobilize. Tiffany, who until now had been standing aside looking baffled, reached for the microphone, but Ivy dodged her and slid away.

"You know those girls who always seemed to get away with everything that no one else could get away with? The girls who wielded their power and money over the school as if *they* were running the place?"

Ivy continued, pacing. "Well, guess what? This year they were finally caught. They were finally going to be brought to justice. But shocker of all shockers, they wrangled a deal. If they make five million dollars tonight, their precious house will not be dissolved, as it should have been long ago. See, they're using people again to get what they want. More specifically, they're using you and your hard-earned money to save their own skins. Is that what you want? Haven't the Billings Girls done enough damage already?"

My heart was in my toes. First Josh and now this. I looked wildly around at the esteemed guests and tried to find Josh. Tried to see his reaction to this, to see if he'd known this was coming, but I was unable to focus on any one face. All I could see was a lot of nodding and pinched expressions. All I could hear were knowing whispers. Her words were hitting home. This was working. Her evil plan was working.

"Reed! Do something!" Vienna said through her teeth.

"You have to get up there. Stop her," London added, letting go of my arm.

But I was frozen. My throat was dry. My head a complete fog. "I . . . I can't. I can't."

This was it. This was the beginning of my nervous breakdown. Ivy had won. She had won Josh. She had destroyed Billings. Destroyed me. And I was so shaken, so broken, so crushed, that I couldn't think of a single word to stop her.

"For years, the women of Billings have been making our lives a living hell," Ivy continued, "but we can end this now. Don't give them your money! Don't support the hypocrisy!"

"Omigod, enough. Reed! You have to shut her up," Vienna said.

Then she shoved me forward so hard I almost tripped into the stairs that led to the stage. Tiffany couldn't have looked more relieved to see me, but Ivy simply smirked.

"Oh, look, it's Reed Brennan, president of Billings," she said as she sneered down her nose at me. "I don't know about the rest of you, but I'm dying to hear what she has to say in her defense."

Hundreds of pairs of eyes turned to me. I was frozen in terror.

"Come on up, Reed! What are you waiting for?"

Ivy descended two steps, grabbed my arm, and dragged me up next to her, practically dislocating my shoulder. She shoved the microphone into my hand and stepped back. A cold sweat broke out all over my body. I stared out at the crowd, but all I could see were Josh's lips on Ivy's, Cheyenne's dead body on the floor, her name in my in-box ten thousand times over, the note, the black marbles, the perfume bottle, the stain on the sleeve of the pink sweater. All of it. All of it reeled through my mind at a sickening speed. I was so dizzy, so disoriented, so confused, I actually reached for Ivy for support, but she flinched away and I almost went down.

"Oops. I think our hostess might be a little buzzed," Ivy shouted, amused.

Somehow I righted myself, but the laughter her comment elicited stung every inch of my skin. What was I doing here? Why were all these people looking to me? I didn't belong here. I was nobody. I was just a loser from Pennsylvania who had been dumped and stalked and nearly driven out of my mind.

This was it. This was where it all fell apart.

"I'm sorry," I blurted out of nowhere. "I'm sorry, I—"

And then a strong hand came down on my shoulder. I sensed it was Noelle before I even saw her. She reached around me, slipped the microphone right out of my hand, and stepped to the front of the stage.

"Thank you, Ivy, for the unplanned entertainment," she began with a smile, coaxing out a few laughs from the crowd. "For those of you who don't know me, I'm Noelle Lange, and I am a senior at Easton Academy and at Billings House. I just want to go on the record as saying that almost everything Ivy has just told you . . . is true."

There were a few gasps and some stunned silence. No one was expecting that. I stepped back and hugged my now freezing-cold arms. Watched her as if I was watching a film, a play—something from which I was completely detached.

"Our living arrangements were put in jeopardy due to some unfortunate incidents earlier this year, true, and it is also true that we asked Headmaster Cromwell for a second chance," Noelle continued. "He agreed that the best way for us to prove our loyalty to Easton would be for us to throw a fund-raiser for the school and so, here we are. Just to clear things up, you should know that any money you donate this evening will be going directly to the Easton Academy board of trustees, to be used at their discretion. Billings will have no further involvement with the funds."

She glanced at Ivy, who looked angry enough to spit. But she stayed where she was, as if waiting for her next opening. Not that Noelle was about to give her one.

"Now, as for the accusations about the behavior of the Billings Girls, all I can say is, Ivy is right," Noelle continued. "We have, in the past, used our power and position on campus to get the things we wanted, but all that has changed this year. This year's new house members were chosen by the administration, not by the residents of Billings. They were chosen for their academic merit, their service to the school, their morals and standards. They are the best of what Easton has to offer."

She looked down at our friends, who had now gathered in front of the stage, like a mother hen looking down at her freshly hatched chicks.

"They deserve a chance to make Billings what it should be," Noelle continued. "They shouldn't have to pay for the crimes, whether real or perceived," she said, pointedly looking at Ivy, "of those of us who came before.

"They are the new Billings, and the new Billings is about sister-hood, about strength, about doing what's right and putting forth the best image we can for Easton," Noelle continued. "That's where your hard-earned money is going tonight. To building a better Billings, a better Easton, a better future." She paused and looked around the room, driving her message home to each and every member of her audience. "Are you really going to let one misguided party crasher get in the way of all that?" she asked, lifting a blithe hand toward Ivy.

The laughter and applause filled the room this time, and we all knew. We all knew that Noelle had won. She handed the microphone to Tiffany, who quickly squirreled it away. Ivy simply stood there, arms crossed in an indignant pose, until she finally shook her head and made her retreat. The cheers were still echoing in my head when Noelle turned to me. There was no way to express the force of gratitude that was surging through my weakened body.

"Noelle, thank you so much," I gushed, a tear spilling down my cheek. "I didn't know what to do. I—"

"Well, Glass-Licker. Looks like I've saved your little fund-raiser twice now," Noelle interrupted, her eyes flashing. "I guess you were right all along. This *is* my house."

I felt like she had just slapped me across the face. "What?" I gasped.

Noelle looked me up and down like I was some pile of dog doo she'd just stepped in, and strode right past me. What was going on? Had she planned this all along? *Had* she booked the St. Sebastian behind my back? Did she have the makeover and photo shoot plan up her sleeve from the beginning? Sabine was right. Noelle had been working against me. And I had let her in. I had let myself believe she cared about me—that we were friends. But Noelle had no idea what it meant to be a friend. All she cared about was herself.

"How could you?" I blurted, whirling around. "How could you do this to me?"

Noelle paused and half turned. She had her iPhone in her hand and shook her head, laughing as she looked down at it. "Funny. I was about to ask you the same thing," she spat.

She thrust the phone in my face and the entire world screeched to a stop.

Me and Dash. Me and Dash in streaming video on the tiny screen. Kissing. Touching. Falling down on a red mattress together. My hands groping for his waistband. His fingers unzipping my dress. It was all there. All of it. My night at the Legacy. She had seen it all.

ON THE OUTSIDE

Noelle headed for the door, but for the first time all night I knew what I had to do. I had to stop her. I had to make her understand.

"Noelle, please! Please, stop. Let me explain!"

I chased her down, grabbed her arm. She yanked it away with so much force she almost knocked me off my feet.

"This is the Legacy!" she snapped, her hands shaking as she held up the phone. "This is the night Dash and I got back together."

I couldn't tear my eyes away from the video. It had been taken from the entrance to the tent. Who had done this? How? Was it Ivy? Was it someone spreading gossip? Why? And why had they sent it to her now?

"Don't you have anything to say, Miss Trust-Me? Miss I-Can't-Lose-You-Too?" Noelle demanded, trembling with anger. "God, to think I called you my sister!" she spat. "You're nothing but a back-stabbing, lying slut!"

A few people around us gasped, reminding me that we weren't alone. Reminding me of where we were.

"Noelle, I am so, *so* sorry," I choked out, approaching her with tears streaming down my face.

"Hell, yeah, you're sorry," Noelle replied under her breath, getting as close to me as possible. Clearly she didn't want any members of the audience she had just won over to hear what she had to say. "You're done at Billings, Reed. Done at Easton. You may as well pack your shit up and hop the next train back to Croton, because you are not going to want to be around to find out what I can do to you."

I looked around, desperate . . . for what? An ally? Someone to swoop in and save me? Someone to take my side? Where was Sabine? Where were Constance and Tiffany and Rose? As my eyes searched, I saw that half the people in the vicinity were watching us, while the other half were looking at their phones. Looking and laughing. Gasping. Pointing at me. Whoever had sent the video had sent it not only to Noelle, they had sent it to all of Easton. Scorching humiliation rushed through me, burning me from the inside out. My life was over.

I had to get out of here. Now.

Stumbling like I was inebriated, I groped my way blearily toward the exit. There were a few people near the door, getting their coats, and they all shied away from me as if I were somehow contagious. I fumbled through my purse for my ticket, grabbed my coat, and turned to go. That was when I spotted Constance, standing in the hallway, talking to Marc, their heads bent together.

Relief rushed through me. Constance. Yes. She was my friend. She had always been loyal. She would help me now. Listen. Understand.

"Constance, thank God," I said, walking over to them. "I can't believe this is happening."

When she looked up at me, her face was pale. "I can't believe you did this," she said, her voice weak, her eyes betrayed. "You and Noelle are supposed to be friends. And you and Josh were still together that night, weren't you? How could you do this to him? To them? What kind of person are you?"

"Wh-what?" I gasped.

"Reed, I think you should go," Marc told me firmly.

"But, Marc, I—"

"Seriously, before this gets any uglier than it already has," he said, a look of disgust in his normally kind eyes.

They weren't going to forgive me. Two of the kindest people I knew had no interest in hearing my side. That was when I knew for sure that I had no one. It really was over. Just like that. From this moment on I would once again be on the outside, looking in.

IVY TALKS

Outside, the air was frigid. My tears froze to my face and my skin tightened. My head pounded as if someone was using a sledgehammer to find their way through my skull to my brain. I caught the disturbed glances of a few passersby and tried to breathe. I had to focus. Had to figure out my next move. But I couldn't even remember what street I was on. All my things were back in Noelle's room. Where was I going to stay tonight? How would I get back to Easton?

A yellow cab pulled up at the curb and out stepped Dash McCafferty. I stared at him like he was some kind of mirage as he paid the driver and turned around. He wore a black coat over his tux, making him appear even broader than usual, and his hands were ensconced in black leather gloves. It took a moment for him to see me, but when he did, he hustled right over.

"Reed, what are you doing out here?" he asked, glancing past me at the door. "I'm so sorry I'm late. There was this whole thing with my sister and her husband and . . ."

He finally looked at my face. "Crap. Is Noelle really pissed?" Um, there was the understatement of the millennium.

"Dash, she knows," I said shakily.

A shadow crossed his face, and I was certain he understood me completely. Yet he asked, "Knows what?"

"About us. About the Legacy," I said, my voice growing louder and shriller with each word. "They *all* know." I threw my hand out toward the door. "Someone videotaped it and just sent it to the entire student body."

"What?"

He looked at the door again, his face growing ashen. He started to compulsively grip his hands together. He was contemplating whether or not to go inside. I could tell. Did he want to face Noelle and her wrath, or would she be even more furious if he never showed? I almost felt sorry for him, having to face such a dilemma.

"I can't believe this is happening," I heard myself say.

"Come on." He turned and took my upper arm in his hand, his grip firm and steadying. "I'm going to get you home."

The words were like music to my ears. Someone was on my side. Someone was willing to help me. But it was the wrong someone. The only someone whose help I could not accept. It took every ounce of willpower left in my wrecked body to pull away from his comforting warmth.

"No. You can't. I can't be seen with you. Especially not now," I said. "You'd better just go. If anyone sees us out here talking like this, it'll just make things worse."

Dash's jaw clenched. He so wanted to do the chivalrous thing, I knew. That was who he was.

"Reed, I'm so sorry," he said quickly, quietly. "Did you get my e-mail? You never responded."

His e-mail. Right. For the first time in days I wondered what he had said. But then the door behind him opened and out poured a few familiar people from school, all laughing and carefree.

"You have to go, Dash. Please," I begged.

Dash glanced at the Easton crowd and rolled his shoulders back. "You're sure you're okay?"

"Yes. Just go."

Reluctantly, he turned. My heart panged at the sight of his back, knowing I was letting one of my last friends leave.

"And Dash?" I said.

He paused.

"Good luck. With her, I mean," I said.

His jaw clenched as he turned his head slightly so that I could see his profile. "You too."

He ducked his head and hurried off down the sidewalk. A stiff wind nearly blew me over and I lifted the collar of my jacket. I should have taken Dash's cab. Not that I would have known how to pay for it. I'd left my cash back at Easton, thinking I'd have no use for it this weekend. Stupid, stupid, stupid.

"Guess now you know how it feels."

My blood curdled at the sound of Ivy's voice. I turned around and found her standing behind me, bundled into a puffy white fur jacket. God, I could have strangled her. Could have just taken out everything on that skinny neck of hers.

"How what feels?" I said through my teeth.

"The dark side of Billings," she said with a knowing smile. Slowly, she walked toward me, her high heels crunching on the sidewalk. "I know you've been asking around about me. Ever heard of the saying 'Curiosity killed the cat'?"

Suddenly a rush of realization warmed my face. Ivy had taken that video. I knew now for sure. She hadn't wanted me to attend the Legacy, had been pissed when I'd let her know I was there. This was her revenge. It had to be. It had to have been her.

Her light blue eyes, so much like Ariana's, bored into mine and I was chilled to the core. What else was this girl capable of? And why did the city street suddenly seem so very deserted?

"You want to know about me and Billings, Reed? Fine. I'll tell you about me and Billings," she said, placing her hands in her pockets. "Back when we were sophomores, Cheyenne and I were best friends—had been since we were little—but you knew that already, didn't you? Snoop that you are."

My teeth clenched. I wanted to call her out so badly. How dare she act like my snooping was so offensive when she'd been in my room half a dozen times? When she'd been stalking me, torturing me, making me feel trapped in my own dorm. But I kept my mouth shut. I wanted to hear this. Had to hear this.

"She knew she was getting into Billings as a legacy, and even though I couldn't have cared less, when I got my invite she told me I had to join. We would room together, be Billings Girls together. She was so excited about it I couldn't say no."

Ivy wandered over to an evergreen tree in a planter in front of the building and reached out to toy with its needles.

"So I went through their stupid hazing rituals for her, stole tests and snuck into the guys' dorms and all that crap, all for her," she continued, her eyes losing focus as she stared at the tree. "Back then one of their tasks was to break into a house and steal a pre-selected artifact. Cheyenne was a legacy, so they gave her an easy task—go to her own house in Litchfield and bring back Rinnan's Golden Globe. Simple. So we did it. All the sophomores together. Me and Cheyenne, Rose, Portia, Taylor, Kiran, et cetera, et cetera. We basically walked right in through the front door and when we came out the juniors and seniors were waiting to congratulate us. But my task wasn't so simple." She looked at me then. "My task was to break into my grandmother's house with its state-of-the-art security system and steal a family heirloom. To this day I don't know how they knew about that stupid box, but that was what they wanted."

So it had been a Billings test. That story I'd found had all been the result of hazing. "Were they trying to keep you out?" I heard myself ask, before I even realized I was going to speak. But I had to know. It was, after all, what Cheyenne had tried to do to Sabine, Constance, and Lorna earlier this year.

"I don't think so," she conceded. "They didn't know about the security. But I knew it was going to be impossible and I told Cheyenne that. But she wouldn't let me back out. Billings was too important. So we did it. We broke in. And even though I tried to plan it carefully, we tripped an alarm." She snorted derisively. "That place was like Fort Knox. My father had insisted on it, since my grandmother had insisted on living alone. I was in my grandmother's room when the alarm went off. Had that stupid box in my hand and everything when she woke up terrified and keeled over onto the floor, right at my feet."

She had spaced again, looking off into the distance.

"All my supposed sisters came in and tried to drag me out of there, but at that point I was on the floor trying to help my grandmother," she continued. "They were all panicked, so one by one they all fled. Then suddenly Noelle and Ariana were there, and Ariana was telling me we had to go. The cops were coming. That we were screwed if we stayed. And Cheyenne was behind them bawling, begging me to go with them. But what was I supposed to do? Leave my grandmother alone there to die? When it was my fault?"

Ivy's eyes shone with unshed tears and she glared at me as if I had been there too. As if I had been playing Ariana's role, telling her to save her own skin. To save Billings instead of her grandmother.

"Noelle kept telling me that my grandmother would be fine. That the police were already on their way and that they would take care of her. Like she cared," Ivy said with a scoff. "But I knew better. I knew she didn't care about anyone but herself. So I told her to go. To get the hell out and leave me there with my grandma. And you know what? That's exactly what she and the others did. Even Cheyenne."

"She did care," I said flatly, automatically defending Noelle. "She was trying to make sure you didn't get in trouble on top of everything else. It wasn't just about saving herself."

"She really has you under her thumb, doesn't she?" Ivy said with an almost sad smirk. "Did you even hear what I just said? They left me there. Alone. To potentially watch my grandmother die. Cheyenne even grabbed the silver jewelry box they wanted me to get. It was all about completing the task. All about impressing Billings."

I had a sudden flash in my mind of that box I had found in Cheyenne's room. The silver box with the engraving on the top of the initials *V.M.S.* That must have been the box. Ivy's family heirloom. *S* for Slade. Cheyenne had actually kept it all this time. How had she lived with that thing in her sight? How had the guilt of what she'd done to her best friend not torn her apart?

"So I was the only one who got arrested that night, though my father had the charges dropped later," Ivy continued, standing up straight and facing me again. "And last year I went to school in Boston so I could help care for my grandmother, but she was never the same again. The whole family was relieved when she finally passed on this summer, saying she had gone to a better place, but at the funeral no one could even look at me. They all blame me, and they should. It's my fault she's gone. Billings's fault."

In spite of myself my heart actually went out to her right then. I couldn't imagine the pain of what she'd been through. How it must have felt to know what she had done. How awful. How incredibly awful.

"So that, Reed, is why I hate Billings. Why I hate Ariana. Why I hated Cheyenne. Why I still hate Noelle," she said, stepping closer to me, getting right in my face. "Ariana, she made her own bed, but Noelle . . . Noelle is still there. Still walking around like she's God's gift, lording her power over everyone. But I know what she really is. What she's capable of. That's why I'll do anything to see the ivory tower fall. *Anything.*"

A blast of cold shot through me, even though the air was now still. Any sympathy I'd felt for her a second ago was blown away.

Ivy had killed Cheyenne. Cheyenne's parents were right. Their daughter hadn't committed suicide. She had been murdered. By her former best friend.

Suddenly, it all made sense. I already knew Ivy had figured out a way to get into Billings, since she'd been torturing me for weeks. She must have sneaked in that night and somehow orchestrated Cheyenne's suicide in order to get back at her for choosing Billings over her, for leaving her there all alone with her ailing grandmother. Then Ivy had decided to release her venom on me—the house's other leader, the new symbol of Billings. She hated us. Hated all of us. And if that look in her eye was any indication, she was capable of murder.

And now she had singled out Noelle. What did that mean? Was Noelle her next victim? Was that how she was going to make the so-called ivory tower fall?

The door behind Ivy opened and Josh stepped through, buttoning up the last button on his coat. He glanced at me quickly, but then looked away, as if it pained him to look me in the eye.

"There you are," he said, slipping his hand into Ivy's. "You ready to get out of here?"

I stared at their entwined fingers. He was holding the hand of a murderer. My Josh. My love. Holding hands with evil.

Ivy looked at me triumphantly, smiled, and said, "Definitely."

Josh shot me one last look as they turned to go, but in my state of miserable panic, I couldn't read it. Was he disappointed? Angry? Sad? Indifferent? I had no idea. All I knew was that I had to get him away from her. I had to save him. But how? I opened my mouth to speak, to shout some kind of warning, but they were already ten paces away, and before I could get a word out, Ivy turned her head and looked back at me. She looked back at me with a flicker in her eye that stopped me dead. A look that scared me so badly it took the breath right out of me. And then they turned at the corner and were gone.

Traffic whizzed by me on the avenue and a cold rain started to fall. Josh was gone. Dash was gone. There was no one left. No one to tell what I now knew about Ivy. No one to help me figure out what to do.

I was in this alone.

From bestselling author
KATE BRIAN

❤❤❤❤❤

Juicy reads for the sweet and the sassy!

Sweet 16
As seen in *CosmoGIRL*!

Lucky T
"Fans of Meg Cabot's *The Princess Diaries* will enjoy it." —*SLJ*

Megan Meade's Guide to the McGowan Boys
Featured in *Teen* magazine!

The Virginity Club
"*Sex and the City: High School Edition.*" —*KLIATT*

The Princess & the Pauper
"Truly exceptional chick-lit." —*Kirkus Reviews*

FROM SIMON PULSE
❤ Published by Simon & Schuster ❤